Thomas Edward Brown

The Manx Witch

And other Poems

Thomas Edward Brown

The Manx Witch
And other Poems

ISBN/EAN: 9783337206925

Printed in Europe, USA, Canada, Australia, Japan

Cover: Foto ©Andreas Hilbeck / pixelio.de

More available books at **www.hansebooks.com**

THE MANX WITCH

AND OTHER POEMS

BY

T. E. BROWN

AUTHOR OF 'BETSY LEE,' 'FO'C'S'LE YARNS,' ETC.

London

MACMILLAN AND CO.

AND NEW YORK

1889

CONTENTS

First comes Tom Baynes among these sorted quills,
In asynartete octosyllables.
Methinks you see the " fo'c's'le " squat, the squirt
Nicotian, various interval of shirt,
Enlarged, contract—keen swordsman, cut-and-thrust :
Old salt, old rip, old friend, Tom Baynes comes *fust*.

Succeeds our Curate, innocent and good,
The growth of Oxford in her sanest mood ;
Dame Nature's child, though bred among the Stoics,
And, if he gush, he gushes in heroics.
Forgive the youth if sometimes he relax
In extra gush of pseudo-dochmiacs.

Last hear our Pazon, reverend and meek ;
In unadornéd verse I make him speak,
As is most fit.   To him Tom Baynes' rude style
Were " simply barbarous "—I see him smile
His smile—" Poor Tom has thoughts beyond his station,
But language ! sir—unfit for publication."
The Curate's rhymes he haply thinks audacious,
Emphatic, overwrought.   " But 'twere ungracious
Of me to criticise a gentleman
That is so kind and clever."   There again
You have our *Pazon*.   So he says his say,
And all my dreams of Manxland fade away.

T. E. B.

Clifton, April 1889.

THE MANX WITCH

A STORY OF THE LAXDALE MINES

THE Pazon that overtook her there
Comin home from Hollantide fair—
The Pazon? No, but Nessy Brew—
Overtook her at Follieu,
Past Bibaloe—aye, man, aye—
Middlin near the Never-say-die—
Toplisses—you'll know the spot—
Nessy Brew though, whether or not—
Nessy—her of coorse that had been
At the fair—The Pazon? navar was seen,
Nor navar could be at the like of yandhar—
Pazon Gale ! you goosie-gandhar—

What are you thinkin of? Navar! navar!

Some people's got a notion they're clavar—

Witty—eh? But navar mind.

Cryin? most despard! cryin, cryin,

Cryin fit to break her heart,

The Pazon was sayin ; and her that smart,

Of a rule, and noways apt to be freckened [1]

Night or day.

        So the Pazon reckoned

She must have got in some trouble, and hauls

Ould Smiler back in the breeches, and calls ;

And "Nessy," he says, "is that you?

It's Nessy, isn't it? Nessy Brew?"

Dark, you know, and drizzlin rain—

But Nessy wouldn answer again

For a bit don't ye see? lek didn want

The Pazon to know her, and made a slant,

And stoopin there, and in on the ditch.

But the Pazon gave a little *skitch*,

And got in front, and pinned her as nate

As possible, and

            "You're very late

     [1] Frightened.

On the road," he says—and *wacin and woin*—

And—" How are you on the road alone?

Extrorn'ry!" says the Pazon—" What!

Alone!" he says—and this and that,

But kind—aw bless ye! kind thallure [1]—

And—" Nessy, Nessy, to be sure!"

And—" Get up, and tell me all aburrit." [2]

So Nessy seen there was nothin for it

But up she must in the Pazon's gig:

And then she tould him all the rig—

Well—maybe not all—not raisonable—

A gel, you know—they're hardly able—

Aisy! aisy with the lek!

All! God bless ye! you musn expeck—

And talkin to a Pazon—eh?

And didn know hardly what to say,

But tould him—Says she, " I didn lave Doolish [3]

Alone at all;" and rather foolish

She was feelin of coorse, aw sartinly—

"There was two people tuk the road with me,"

Says Nessy. " Two," says the Pazon, " aw dear!

And did you meet them in the feer?" [4]

---

[1] Enough.   [2] About it.   [3] Douglas.   [4] Fair.

"The feer? says Nessy, "no—at laste
It might ha' been—a nisy place
In a field," she says, "there was hosses there—
Is that what people is callin the feer?
Hosses, and gingerbread, and pop,
And cows, and calves   but I didn stop."
"Didn ye?" says the Pazon then :
"And was it two women, or was it two men
You tuk the road with?"   Aw, not a word
From Nessy.   "I think," says the Pazon, "I heard
Your friends down there on the Whitebridge hill."
"Aw," says Nessy, "are they fightin still?"
"No," says the Pazon, "they warn together,
One was far ahead of the other,
Shoutin though, the two of them—
Yes, I think it ll be the same :
And you'll 'scuse me," he says—sittin up like a crowbar
Was the Pazon then   "they were hardly sober,
Hardly, he says; and then his vice
Gies a little *hem!* like puttin a splice
On his kind ould throat   "a little," he says,
"A little to icated   yes
A little, I think ; a little queer :

And usin language, I think they were,
Language—aye—"

     " They were fightin," says Nessy,
" When I left them—aw messy ![1] messy ! "
She says, " they've lost one another, that's it,
Lost they have, and 'll hommer and hit
And grab in the dark there, and navar get hould,
And 'll take and get their death of could—
Oh dear ! oh dear ! " and began a sabbin.
" I suppose this homm'rin and hittin and grabbin
Is about a young woman called Nessy Brew,"
Says the Pazon. " Oh ! they'd come for you,"
Says Nessy, " they'd come for you they wud ; "
And " Aw the muck ! and aw the blood !
Yes, sir, aw yes, sir ! aw poor Jack—
And Harry too—" And—" Let's turn back ! "

" And why did you lave them ? " says the vicar ;
And—" The two of them," she says, " in liquor ;
And I thought, sir, I thought, when they hadn me,
It's peacefuller they'd be sure to be,
And helpin each other, and takin rest,[2]

---

  [1] Mercy.   [2] Pacified.

And forgettin me." —"Aw, indeed," he says,
" Forgettin you then—aw the poor chile !"
And he smiled, and bless ye ! you'll feel a smile
In the dark—" forgettin, and lost the bearins—
Poor thing ! and have you got your fairins
In your handkecher ?   And—" Yes."   " All right !"
Says the Pazon, " you'll not see these young men to-night
Again," he says ; so -" Come up, Smiler !"
And away, and tryin to reconcile her.

But scoulded a little too, and *How*
Did the father ever go and allow
The like of her, that hadn no call,
To be goin to Hollantide fair at all ?
But goin by herself ?   " I went with my aunt,
Says Nessy.   "She's a woman that's scant
Of prudence," says the Pazon, says he—
" Billy's widow—and where is she ?"
" I think she's tuk at these poleeses,"
Says Nessy.   " There's aunts that's worse till their meeces,"
The Pazon said ; *and indeed he'd spake*
To her father, he said.   *Aw the sake ! the sake !*
And be certin he wouldn.   " I owe it," he says,

"To your father," *the good-naturedest,*
The simplest man that ever he knew—
"Poor Brew!" he says, "poor Jemmy Brew!"

And then he spoke though, terble nice—
Aw the beautiful advice!
Delicake though, delicake—
Aw that was the Pazon, bide or break.
But when they came to the steep hill
At the Cloven Stones, "Sit still, sit still!"
Says the Pazon, and down on his tippitoes,
And a hould of Smiler by the nose,
And leadin, and thinkin, *and how he must warn her,*
And "serious very!" turns Kelly's corner
At the bottom yandhar, and a stip and a step,
And a heave and a plump, and where was this rep?[1]

Maybe a mile aback on the road
By gough! and him that navar knowed—
Tuk her opportunity,
Slipt out, and away, of coorse to see
Could she find these chaps, aw, I'll be bail—

---

[1] Rip.

"The little monkey!" says Pazon Gale.

Aw, bless ye! I've heard him tellin

Another Pazon, ould Pazon Gellin,

That was on St. Mark's, I did, I did,

Yes, and shakin his dear old head:

" And I'm not in the habit of the lek,

Mr. Gellin," he says, "and you'd hardly expeck,

But tuk like that, and the way she'd fled,

I called her a little monkey!" he said.

Little she wasn, no! doodoss![1]

But aw the funny the Pazon was!

Good though, good ; aw, bless your heart !

That's the timber 'll navar start.

'Bout ship, sir! aye immadient,

And then this poor ould reverend gent,

Backards and forrards the best of the night

Drivin there, a most shockin sight,

If he could ha' been seen ; but made up his mind

At last to go on to Ballaquine,

Brew's form that was lyin east,

Far beyond the Pazon's place,

By Jove (or some such expletive.

And *he'd tell the father and see would he go*
To look for his daughter himself . . . and so

Off with him straight, and hardly awake—
Aw, bless ye! the day was begun to break,
And—Mrs. Gale—aw well of coorse,
And nathural, and shuttin the doors
Every night at nine o'clock ;
And let a man be as studdy as a rock,
And a Pazon too, but still, dear me!
Lookin terble like on the spree—
Backard and forrard, and niddin and noddin,
Just like ould Jemmy Ballavoddin—
And the Misthress——

                    Well, I'll say no more,
But up with him there and slams at the door
With the end of his whip, and *hurroose! hurroo!*
Jemmy! James! Mr. Brew! Mr. Brew!
And Jemmy to put his head out of the windy,
And—*Bless his sowl! and what was the shindy?*
And—"Is Nessy at home?" says the Pazon then :
Nessy at home! "Why—— Nessy ven!"[1]

___
[1] Dear.

Nessy! goodness grayshers! Pazon—

Nessy at home! a queer thing to be as'in;

D'ye think she's out agate o' the priddhars[1]

As arly as this?"   So the Pazon considhars

A bit, and—"Call her then," he said,

"Call her."—"Nessy, ger up urrov[2] bed,

And spake to the Pazon—funny work!"

And shuts the windhar with a jerk.

   And then another windhar went down,

And out come a bunch of curls as brown

As a nut, and a face as fresh as a rose,

And just the smallest taste of clothes,

And the sun all dabbin her like fire,

And looks at the Pazon as modest—"Retire,

Retire," says the Pazon; "that 'll do, that 'll do,"

And not another word to Brew

Nor the daughter neither; but turns the hoss,

And home with him.   It wasn cross

He was lookin, no! but sad though, sad,

I ck orrowful, lek a way he had.

---

[1] Potatoe.   [2] Out of.

Aye, but Brew was puzzled greatly,

Bless ye! he was beat complately—

The Pazon wand'rin about in the dark

Of a Hollantide night—a 'stonishin lark,

Wantin Nessy before she was up!

Dear me! Could he have had a sup,

Or what? but no! unpozzible—

The Pazon—aye there's some of them will,

No doubt! no doubt! but drinkin! him!

Aw, bless your granny! sink or swim,

That was the Pazon—

                "What cud it ha' been,

Nessy?" he says, "I navar seen

The lek," he says: "was it walkin he was

In his sleep, or drivin, at laste, and the hoss

Tuk for the Ballaquine on a chance?"

But no! God bless him! there wasn no sense

In that; and the late or the arly—which?

And beat all conscience and as dark as pitch

The most of the time—and

                "Nessy gel,

What could he be wantin? Was he lookin unwell?

But my goodness grayshers! just to ax

Were you up, and then to be makin tracks
Lek immadient there—d'ye see!
And no satisfaction for nobody.
And Smiler—aye—nearly druv off his legs—
What could it be, Nessy?"

      " Maybe eggs,"

Says Nessy—" Yes, he's thinkin a dale
Of our fresh eggs is Pazon Gale—
Tould me so."—" Aw dear, that's rum,"
Says Brew, "and why didn ye give him some?"
" Because he didn ax," says she—
" Ax? is it ax?" and " Fiddledee!
Eggs! woman, eggs! it couldn ha' been—
Bless my sowl! the man 'd be keen
For his eggs that 'd come that arly—eh?
Nessy, Nessy.'   " Well, anyway,"
Says Nessy, "the Pazon's allis talkin
About our eggs: 'They're nice though shockin,'
He was sayin, 'just like wax.'"
" My goodness grayshers! why didn he ax?"
Says the father.   " Maybe he forgot,"
Says Nessy.   Then Brew got middlin hot,
And " You're just talkin nonsense," he says, "be quite,

Not another word ! "

Then he laughed outright

When he thought of the Pazon and the way he cut,

And then he gev a little *chut !*[1]

And "I have it !" he says, "it's Copper, guy heng !"[2]

Copper ! that's the very theng ! "

Copper—a mailie[3] cow that was arrim,[4]

Three cows, I think, not much of a farrim,[5]

More like a croft, or the like of that—

"Copper—that's what he was at :

And knew I was wantin to sell her—eh ?

But couldn go with her anyway

To the fair—that accounts for this scarum-scorum,[6]

Freckened some would be before him—

That's the arly—— dear me !

The anxious lek the man must be—

It'll come in the price, aw 'deed it will—

He's hot upon her—she's very lill,[7]

But good uncommon—twelve I'll take for her,

Twelve pound ten."—" And why didn he spake for her?

---

[1] Tut (interjection).

[2] A harmless kind of oath. [3] Without horns. [4] At him, that he had.

[5] Farm. [6] Eccentric conduct. [7] Little.

Surely he might have axed," says she.
" I suppose he forgot it."—" Fiddlededee!"
Says Nessy —" Like the eggs," says Brew,
And *he-he-he* and *hoo-hoo-hoo*—
They laughed and they laughed—"forgot!" "forgot!"
" Like the eggs," "like the cow," like the—— go to pot!
" Forgot, no doubt, forgot!" and as merry
The two of them there—aw very, very.

That night I was up at the Ballaquine;
And there was Nessy, and Sally Behind—
The aunt, you know, a widow woman,
And a sister of Brew's, that was imprint uncommon,
And bad with the tongue; she was goin a-callin
Sally Behind, for the way she was fallin
Abaft of her midships: Manx? yes, Manx,
For all her married name was Banks—
Brew's sister—and the talk that was there!
And the Pazon comin home from the fair
And as drunk! aw bless ye! as drunk as rosin[1]
That was the aunt.   " He wasn! he wasn!"
Says Nessy, " no such a thing!"—" And how

___
[1] (Probably an allusion to the convivial habits of fiddlers).

Do you know?" says the aunt; aw then the row!

My gough! they went at it!

But Jemmy Brew

Was smilin there, and "Hush then! shoo!"

He says; and "Here's a chap with brains—

What's your opinion, Thomas Baynes?"

"My opinion," says I, "it's aisy given—

If ever there was an angel in heaven,

It's Pazon Gale. Did ye ever hear,"

Says I, "of angels the wuss for beer?

Gerr[1] out!" I says, "I know his trim,

If you don't, and I'll fight for him,

I'll die for him, I'll be cut in pieces,

And fifty aunts, nor fifty nieces——

But—as'in your pardon, Nessy," I says,

"You've tuk his part—all right! success

To the handsome gel you allis were,

Aye, and gennal[2]—— but that woman there,"

I says, "I think she'd better be cookin

Her own mate," I says, "and lookin

To herself a bit both before and *behind* her—

---

[1] Get.   [2] Genial, kindly.

And look slippy," I says, just a lill reminder,
A sort of a dig d'ye see? woahup!
Look out for squalls! My gough! She up
With a clout, and made a drive that vicious
She didn strike me, but she knocked two dishes
And a pazil¹ of plates there off the dresser;
And the niece to shout *whatavar'd possess her*
To do such jeel with the crockery
Of ither people—very free,
Very—and batthar remember the cost—
And it wasn her house

                 And no more it was;
For she lived in a thalthan² up the river
Belongin to Brew that wouldn have her
In the house with him at all—no, he wudn!
Not even when the wife died, which died very sudden,
And Nessy only a child—no, no!
So I thought it was just about time to go—
But I stood for the Pazon—aw, cut and thrust!
Ye see, I was lovin him scandalous
Aye and everybody—and no thanks!
Only this craythur—this Mrs. Banks—

   ¹ Peck.   ² Half-ruined cottage.

She didn love him, and she didn hate him,
And she knew she couldn aggravate him
No more till a magpie, or a sparrer—
But just the dirty tongue that was arrer [1]—
A miser'ble thing, that deserved to be skelpit—
Only it's lek she couldn help it.

Now what d'ye think this Nessy had done
That Hollantide night, the time she run
And left the Pazon?. There was one of these parties
She never seen, for, behould ye ! my hearties
Tuk diffrin roads, the one to the shore,
And the one to the mountain above Slieu-Core.
So Nessy happened on the track
Of the mountain beauty—and that was Jack—
Jack Pentreath—aw Manx thallure [2]—
But his father was Cornish to be sure—
Neddy St. Ives they were callin the father,
But Jack—aw Jack—that was flighty rather—
Jack Pentreath—well, no, I'll not say
Flighty either ; but ye see the way
It was—but hould on, you'll hear, you'll hear.

[1] At her, was hers.　　　　[2] Enough.

The other chap was Harry Creer—
From Dalby he came, and so he was gettin [1]
" Harry from Dalby."

        Well, Jack was sweatin
Up the mountain, and a hullabaloo,
And a quiv'rin and shoutin what would he do,
And *where was this villyan?* and—" Aisy ! aisy ! "
Says Nessy to him, " you needn go crazy—
Come," she says. " And will you go linkin
With me ? " says Jack. " Aw well I'm thinkin
I'd better," says Nessy ; " it'll be more safer,"
And offs with him—aw as tight as a wafer—
Poor Jack ! but the plazed, and the tittle-tattle,
And studdied hisself. For they'd had a battle
Who'd she link with ? and wouldn take rest,
And round and round like compasses—
And her goin duckin under their arms—
Aw bless ye ! trust these lill [2] madarms !
(Lill she wasn) and then they'd got gript
Like the very deuce, and Nessy slipt
To one side, and them two kissin like mad,
Till they found by the whisker who they had—

      [1] Gettin the name of.   [2] Little.

And then—hurroose!

But as nice you navar

Now—aw dear! and leadin him clavar

Down a lane by the Ballacrie,

Just to dodge the Pazon—aye—

That's it, man—*Sithee!* (these cotton-balls [1]) *sithee!* [2]

And comin out at Lewin's smithy,

And heard the gig, and "come!" and besaechin,

And dragged him in there to the praechin

That was in the chapel—

Aw a nice pair!

And the people gave a terble stare—

But Jack was like a cherubim—

That happy—but had to be hoult in the hymn

At [3] Nessy—aye: and the Pazon druv

Past all right.   And then to shove

This Jack to the door, that was smellin of gin,

And makin faces astonishin,

And the light in his eyes — aw she stuck to the
  chap,

And whenever they heard the Pazon's trap,

---

[1] As these factory hands from Lancashire say.

[2] Seest thou.   [3] By.

They tuk for the hedge, or wherever they cud,

And got him home—intarmined[1] she wud—

Intarmined.

    It'd be on the stroke of three

When they fetched his lodgin—not a light to see,

Nor nothin, and all of them in bed ;

But a-side of the house a little shed,

For tools and the lek, and not even a door in,

And just a push, and left him snoorin ;

And home, and the father in bed since seven,

And thinkin she wouldn be after eleven,

But was for all ; but navar knew—

Aw an aisy ould chap was Jemmy Brew.

    Well now, I'll tell you about Harry and Jack—

Aw, dacent fellows, that's a fact.

Jack was lill, and Harry was big,

And sometimes takin a hearty swig,

I tell ye, but dacent fellows enough.

Harry was tall, but Jack was tough ;

Jack was just like pin wire,

Jack was just like made of fire,

            [1] Determined.

Lean and supple, hard as a rock,

A reg'lar little fightin cock.

Harry's hair was just like tow,

Jack's was as black as the wing of a crow,

Jack was sallow and dark o' the skin,

Harry was red astonishin—

Red though, red: so that was the pair,

Jack Pentreath and Harry Creer.

    Now red or yellow, blue or black,

A passionater fellow till Jack

There couldn ha' been—aw desperate!

He'd have it out, he wouldn wait—

He'd have it out whatever it was—

Have it out—no lip nor sauce

Would do for Jack, no chiffin nor chaffin;

Navar bothered much with laughin

Didn Jack—a word and a blow—

Terrible in earnest though,

Perseverin, if you'll understand—

Jack was like two dogs in one,

The dog to hunt, and the dog to fight;

But still he wasn takin delight

In fightin—no; nor wantin to be
Cock-o'-the-mine—

              Stay—let me see—

Did I tell you they were miners? no?
Miners, miners, just so—
Miners the two of them—Laxdale mines,
That's countin terble [1] for the finds,
And the big wheel yandhar. But, however,
Jack could work the fisses clever.
Harry wasn no match for him,
For all the big of body and limb,
Harry 'd fight of coorse, if he had to,
But I don't suppose he was very glad to.

    But Jack, ye see, if he had a desire
To anything, he was nothin but fire
And rage and fury my gough, the sperrit !
And wouldn give in afore he'd gerrit [2]—
Wouldn ! mortal uncomfible
To have daelins with the lek, for they will,
   And they will and they will, and it isn no use ;
Can't help it, it's lek, houldin on like the deuce ;

---

[1] Accounted excellent.   [2] Get it.

Like these bull-dogs, when once they're gript the teeth,
There's nothin 'll slacken them only death.

Uncomfible they are though, shockin,
And so is a bull-dog, takin and lockin
His jaw like a vice.   And special[1] gels—
They can't be thinkin of nothin else
Night or day, the whole of the world
Is nothin but her, and the head goes whirl,
And the heart like a burnin fiery furnace—
That's the chaps that is in earnest,
And no matter the why and no matter the fur[2]
It's her and her and her and her—
Her they must have—they must, they must,
And all the rest is only dust
And dirt.   And the same for everything—
An oar, a pick—but faymales! by jing!
Faymales! aw, bless ye! simply crazy—
That's it—nor they can't nor they won't take it aisy.

Now Harry was a hearty lad,
But terble hard to make him mad
About the lek : he liked a gel—

_____

[1] Especially.   [2] For, wherefore.

Very well—very well—
Liked her—certainly; but if he got vexed,
Or bothered, you know, just on to the next—
That was Harry—much the same
Whatever happened—a sort of cracm
These chaps has got for blood : it's cool
And sweet and that, and, of a rule,
It's not aisy put out, but—liquor—well,
Of coorse, of coorse.   I could hardly tell
Had Jack any blood in him, but when
The craythur was a-fightin, and then
He had plenty of it and to spare,
But difficult to say the where
It was stowed at him.   Harry's was in his face,
All over him was Harry's case.

Aye, but Jack—aw, none of your blubber
At Jack, not him—just Indian-rubber
All over, aw, a bird of the game,
None of your buttermilk, none of your cracm.
Dry, man, dry and the springy hipped,
The reg'lar whalebone ! See him stripped !
That was the thing—aw, belly or back !

See him stripped, and there was Jack.

He was raelly awful, a sort of a shine

Like shells, like—— aw it's no use try'n—

Comin off him—— lek a kind o' brassy—

Lek these yallar images, aye was he.

Lek the blood, ye see, was a sort of a venom,

Or varnish, or vitriol that was in him.

Quick though, quick—for Harry would swing

His arms like a windmill, but Jack would spring

Like a goose's merry-thought, and at ye he'd come

Like a dart, like a wasp, like a rocket by gum!

So there was two of Miss Nessy's beaux—

Miners, I tould ye—but goodness knows

The chaps that was after yandhar gel—

Respectable ? respectable !

I should think so—*respectable* is it ?

Eiras,[1] bless ye ! would be payin their visit

To the Ballaquine—yes, eiras, drapers

From Dhoolish, bless ye ! with their capers,

Foremen, overseers, a cap'n,

Loadin there on the beach, would drap in

Now and then—I've seen the lek.

[1] Heirs.

But, just azackly the way you'll expeck,
The young miners it was that was schamin
To get this Nessy; just like claimin
She belonged to them whoever'd be
The lucky chap—lek proppity,
Lek shares, lek—— swore together to watch
That none of these dandy divils 'd snatch
The prize, the beauty of Ballaquine,
This *rose that had grew at the mouth of the mine.*

That was their talk.   And a sort of a club,
Or a saycret 'ciety, and hub-and-nub,
And sentries just lek souldiers placin,
And takin their turn of a Sunday facin
The chapel, and up the road, and grips,
And officers, and passes – " Lips "
Was the word, I believe, and the counterword—
Well, I forget; but still I've heard—

But   Lips—that's Nessy—the mouth? just so—
Like a puffeck[1] rose in the full blow
Eyes, of coorse, and nice they were- -
Blue   yes, blue; but the most that was there,

[1] Perfect.

I tell ye, couldn see nothin but just
The mouth.   It wasn a sort of a puss,[1]
Puckered and quilted and hemmed and hitched
And gored and eylotted and stitched—
Plenty of it—— reefs and reefs,
And more to come; and then the teefs[2]
All set round—aw I'll be bail
Drew to scale, drew to scale—
The mouth she had—— aw, hit or miss,
For all the world like a big red kiss.

So these chaps was jealous you navar seen,
And had her for a sort of a queen;
But every miner to have his chance,
And whichever she'd chose, the rest at once
To give in, *resign her*, they said, resign her;
But only she must marry a miner.

Aw many's the blade has been tuk and ducked
In the big dam yandhar, or clouted and mucked,
And all his fine clothes a-soakin like runnet,[3]
And navar the wiser who was it that done it;

---

[1] Purse.   [2] Teeth.   [3] Rennet.

Aye, and caught in the dark, and pounded
At these divils, and navar the one of them rounded
Upon the others—aw true as wedges,
And huntin these drapers over the hedges,
And sthoo'd [1] a chap by the name of Jones
Every step to the Cloven Stones.

Was I in it? ho-ho-ho !
Sailors and miners—bless ye—no !
Wouldn ha' had me, couldn neither—
Differn cattle altogether,
Rovin divils sailors is,
Navar much in the one place :
Besides these miners is more of a clan,
Keepin more on the one hand ;
And I couldn for sartin allis agree with them,
But aisy enough for th'[2] get on the spree with them—
Rather too aisy, for the matter of that ;
But every hatter his own hat,
And every trade its own tricks,
And its own sayerets—nix is nix,
Wherever you'll be.

---

[1] Chased (with opprobrious shouting).   [2] To.

But, houldin their own,

There they had me—— *the rose that had grown*

At the mouth of their mine—— and chaps to be comin

Sniffin and snuffin like bumbees hummin

Around their rose—— it isn raison,

And it isn sense—the same with grazin

On the commons, the same with fishin-ground,

The same with everything; and you're bound

To stick to it too.   And a gel like Nessy—

Dear me! if it was Dick Quayle-vessy,[1]

He's yours for all; look after the lek—

" Cair![2] cair! " says Billy Injebrek.

But a splendid gel like Nessy—chut!

It's nothin but reg'lar poachin : " Cut ! "

Says you to this draper from Dhoolish, " be off!

You Ramsey sneak."   You'd be middlin soft

If you didn—to let them gather your rose

That handy from under your very nose !

" She's ours," you'd say, " and we mean to keep her."

If he stands to it, hit him a tap on the peeper—

They're not much these dandies—down with the fut !

" Cut ! " says you, and by gough they'll cut.

[1] A notorious idiot.   [2] Property.

So that's the way they'd all combine
For the honour and glory of the mine.
Supposin she didn marry the one o' them
All right, all right! still every man o' them
Had had his chance, and equally
She wouldn be marryin nobody.

Friday is pay-day: one Saturday
I was in at Callow's as you may say,
Lek a little sociable or that;
And a hape of miners; and there they sat
Like a Quakers' meetin, no talkin, no laughin,
Not the smallest taste of chaffin,
Till all of them was in the room,
Bless my sowl! a sort of a gloom
Over the lot.   It'd be very near
A week or so after Hollantide feer,
And every chap, as he tuk his place
On the settle or that, you'd see the rest
Lift up their eye as sollum though,
Lek axin; and him with a sort of a *no*,
And a shake of the head, and out with his clay,
And charges and sucks and draws away.

I was noticin; and Jack, d'ye see,

Come in, and the shake accordantly;

And Harry last; and the whole of them lookin,

But Harry had a pipe arrim[1] smookin,

And navar no shake o' the head they'd get,

But just a little sort of a spit

At[2] Harry.

Now it appears they were signin

Articles—I think there was nine in—

Rules, is it? I don't care—

Rules then—that they'd run it fair;

No chap to take advantage lek

Over the rest; and the smallest speck

Lek it would be of encouragement—

Lek a word, or a nod—then this here gent

To kermoonicate it to the lot

Under penalties to be shot,

For all I know, or hung as high

As Haman, if he tould a lie.

Honour bright! I seen the book

Years after, and even a look

---

[1] At him.   [2] On the part of.

Was down, and how much was countin for it.
'Longside the name of the chap that gorrit [1]—
Somethin like—— Jeremiah Wilde—
Looked at him in the chapel, and smiled—
Two marks ; Dick Clucas passin the farrim,[2]
And Nessy hove a priddha [3] arrim.[4]
One mark and a half—— Nathaniel Fathom—
Nessy held the hymn-book with him
Last Sunday, countin seven marks—
Lek that ye know—aw dear, the larks !
Nonsense you're thinkin ?   Aw, lek enough !
But I hardly think ye know the stuff
Them Laxdale chaps is made of, no—
Curious very, treminjis though.

Now it wasn a meetin they had at all,
Lek they're callin it *special general*,
Of the 'ciety, but just drop in
Anybody, and yarns to spin
And talk to talk.   So Harry Creer
Wasn bound to tell them theer
Why he didn shake the head,

---

[1] Got it.   [2] Farm.   [3] Potato.   [4] At him.

Lek meanin nothin done or said

At [1] Nessy to him that week, you know,

But Jack was feelin dreadful low,

For Nessy had spoke to him sure enough,

But terble savage, terble rough,

And the dirty turn-out [2] and sent him flyin,

And he must never come near the Ballaquine—

"Ye nasty thing! you're not fit,

You're no better till a ideit!"

So Jack was mad, and "Come out!" he says—

And terble winkin at the rest—

"Come out!" he says, and as grim as grim;

So out they went, Harry and him.

Aw dear! when he had him out on the street

The row that was at them! I didn see't

Nor nobody, but Harry was tellin—

"What's this?" he says, "what's this, ye villain?"

And a grip of his throat, houldin on like a ferret.

"That's not azackly the way to gerrit," [3]

Says Harry, chokin. "Let go! let go!"

He slackened a bit, but very slow—

---

[1] By.   [2] Repulse, snubbing.   [3] Get it.

Greedy lek—"It wasn much,"
Says Harry, "bless your sowl! don't clutch
Like yandhar—only a handful of gravel
I hove in the window."—"The devil! the devil!"
Says Jack—"you hove—and—well then, well!
She come, she come—aw it's aisy to tell,"
And begun a cryin.   "She come," says Harry,
"Yes, she come, but she didn tarry;
'Harry Creer,' she says, 'the sot,'
And down with the window like a shot."
"Aw Harry, Harry!" and grips his hand,
"Harry, Harry, Harry man!"
And—"Harry, you're a friend of mine;
Keep away from the Ballaquine,
Aw do, la!¹ do! aw yes! aw dear!
You're not lovin her, Harry Creer!
Harry, Harry! just only the pride,
And lek not likin to be put o' one side
When all the chaps is sportin their figures—
Of coorse, of coorse; it's not the biggerst
That's lovin the most, you know it's not,
Harry, you know! aw promise to't!

¹ Interjection of entreaty.

Promise!" and Harry half willin there—

A good-natured sowl. But—"Swear it! swear!

Swear, Harry!" and an oath like your arm

For the long, most despard, like some charm

At these wutches, awful! "Liver and lights"—

Lek cussin all his odd jints—

Till Harry got freckened altogether;

But he didn like to deny him either—

"With blood," says Jack, "with blood, with blood!"

And out with the knife.

                 But Harry stood

Again the notion very stiff,

And—*No, and he didn't like.* "Your shift,"

Says Jack like lightnin, the quick he was—

But Harry gettin rather cross—

"Will you change your shift with Tommy Mawby?"

"Well, what for?" says Harry from Dalby.

"What for?" says Harry—stupid rather.

"Because we'll be up and down together,

And then I'll know where you are," says Jack;

Aw as straight as straight; no keepin back,

No sneakin hoky-poky ways

With yandhar fellow, if you plaze.

Semple, you're thinkin? that may be,—
Love is just semplicity—
Real love, of coorse—chat![1]
Semplicity! why, bless ye! that
Is love, is, is, is, is, or oughter—
Is fire semple? is air? is water?
Semple? "Sincere," the Pazon was sayin—
Sincerity—oh, isn it plain?
One thought, one thought—aw, through and through,
One in her, and one in you—
Semple, single—isn it clear?
Nothin else but just sincere—
A great word with the Pazon—*foolishness?*
No, no, my lads! it's the best thing, the best,
It's the only thing, just the one bright flash
That quivers through this world of trash
And make-believe ; it's swift, it's short,
It's gone— and we're all the better for't,
Aye, and the wiser—couldn stay long,
Not like that　you need to be young
To work that horse-power, mind ye, my men!
Aw yes, you can love again.

[1] Tut.

But not like that—it's only the once—
Aw give it a chance! give it a chance!
One wave flung in upon the shore,
That bursts and breaks for evermore.

So none of your humbug, backin and fillin,
But just straight off—*Would Harry be willin*
To work, you know, on the shift with him,
And then it would be the same trim [1]
For the two of them? "What! navar free
To go by myself?" says Henery,
"And try my luck! lek fastenin us
Together like dogs"—and he gev a cuss—
"I won't," he says.
                    Aw Jack made a run,
And caught him, and gript him, and cryin like fun,
And beggin him for God's sake,
And the tears! the tears! like urrov [2] a lake—
Aw the slush of tears—"Harry, Harry!"
A nice chap for the gel to marry!
The tears then, is it the tears ye mane?
The tears—yes, yes, but comin like rain—

[1] Conditions.   [2] Out of.

There's everything in tears—of coorse !
Look at the pressure, look at the force !
Shallow water? go to pot !
There's shallow water, and there's water that's not.
Pumpin ! says you ; there's some people can,
But the tears of a man that is a man
Is wantin no pumpin, nor no tap, nor no cock,
I know I've got to the real rock
When I see the lek.   You may grin like apes,
You may squeeze your face in a thousand shapes,
You may smooth it till it's like pin-jane,[1]
But the tears, the tears that comes like rain-
Then you have him—see ! he's cryin !
That's the chap ! aw there's no denyin.

And childher—is it only pushin
Their finger that makes the tears come rushin
Till they're nothin but tears, just a livin spout ?
It's because they're turnin inside out
Easier till grown-up people, being pli'ble,
Aye—but us that's ouldher is li'ble
To get hard and stiff, or else all flabby.

[1] Curds-and-whey.

Just a miser'ble sort of drabby,[1]

Lek feelin nothin, or seemin we didn,

Like an ould boot upon a midden.

God bless the childher ! God bless their wayses !

They're spinnin no cobwebs before their faces—

Not much like spiders isn them—

Yandhar David too the same,

In the Bible you've got him, like it appears—

Aw David was the boy for tears !

    I don't hould no more till you

With allis cryin, boo-boo-boo !

Shlishin-slushin, snittle-snottle ;

But " Put my tears in thy bottle,"

Says David, " thy bottle," lek God, it's meant,

Had a bottle arrim,[2] lek fillin with scent,

And like enough a goold stopper—

Aw beautiful ! but must be a whopper

To hould all the tears—a sort of decanter,

Lek silver-mounted—but I wouldn vanture

To say it was really that, but just

To give you a notion, the way we must

---

    [1] Droppy.   [2] At him, in his possession.

With the lek, of coorse, bein what ye may call—
Aye, man, aye—but aisy all!

So Harry couldn stand this cry'n,
And promised there, but he wouldn sign
In blood, no, no!   "It's usual done,"
Says Jack, but didn see the fun,
Didn Harry, but just to be
On the same shift, and glad to get free
Of this chap and all his hollabaloo—
A day shift it was too,
Comin off about five in the everin,
And washed, I tell ye, and as nate as a pin,
And no hurry at all, but the smile on the face,
And plenty of chaps about the place,
Souljerin¹ there, but off on the sly
One after the other   "I think I'll try
Is the troutsis² bitin," they'd say, or bitendin³
To meet the coach, or *had to be mendin*
Something at home: and 'd walk that slack,
And the hands in the pockets, and the swing of the back,
And the slink and the slouch.   But, out of sight,

---

¹ Loafing about.   ² Trouts.   ³ Pretending.

Up to the Ballaquine with them straight—

Hedges and ditches ; but, when they'd get near,

They'd slack again—aw never fear !

And standin and starin very hard

At some oats, or some clover, or a pig in the yard,

Or—anything ; or lookin lek wond'rin

How they come theer at all, and blund'rin

In on the back, and in on the front,

Or the barn, or the haggard ;[1] and a surt of a grunt,

And a heave, and a start, lek " Bless my sowl !

Is this the Ballaquine ? "   And 'd rowl

Their eyes most terble, and amazin to meet

The lot of them theer upon the street.

And the nudgin and shovin there'd be in

For one of them to make a begin

And talk to the gel ; and whichever spoke,

One of the chaps 'd gev a poke

To another, and then the lot 'd buss

Out a laughin, and Nessy would puss

Her mouth, and give a little shy

With her head ; and another chap 'd try,

[1] Stackyard.

And then the roor, and " Woa, man, woa ! "
And " He-he-he," and " Ho-ho-ho ! "

Miners ?   Miners ! sartinly not ;
Miners—they're another lot ;
Miners' soorcyin [1]—aw ye needn doubt it '
They goes another way about it,
Does miners, aye, bein chaps that way,
That's rather for turnin night into day-·
Down in the mines—the way you'd expeck—
Fond of the dark, and used of the lek,
Suckin it just like liquorice-ball,
They can't take up with the daylight at all.

I've heard of people born in a mine,
Poor divils ! aw just as good as blind—
At laste they got no eyes to spake of,
Just a little bit of a strake of
Light, like a groove, like a seam, like a slit,
Livin and dyin in the pit —
That's England —that's these " lower urdhers " [2] —
A despard country, full of murders

---

                [1] Courting.   [2] Orders.

But coals, of coorse, most horrid dirty,
And iron very near as clarty.[1]

   Aye; but in the Isle of Man
It's lead that's goin, you'll understand—
And a dale claner to work it is,
A dale claner—aw 'deed yis!
Claner—but still they had to clane—
Sartinly—you know what I mane—
Titivatin—"In the dark?" says you,
Lek you're thinkin the differ wouldn be knew?[2]
Nonsense! where's a fellow's pluck
To coort, if he's feelin all of a muck,
And sticky and sweaty—no, la! no!
A nice clean shirt and a collar though—
It's what you're feelin, not what you're lookin,
That's the style, or you'd better be hookin.

   And sure enough it's dark they hev[3] it
Often enough; but as right as a trevit,
And comfible that way in your clothes—
Aw it's doin a dale, and goodness knows
Why, but it does; and maybe two'n

---

[1] Filthy.　　　[2] The difference would not be known.　　　[3] Have.

The mornin at ye, a big strong moon
'll swim out of a cloud, and you to stand there
Lookin up, and her in the wandhar
Lookin down—and you like her to see
Your face as bright as a thingummagee,
And your handkecher, and all to that,
Nate, man, nate, and a cock on your hat,
Like a surt of a buck; and look at her—
The clane she is, and the tickelar.

Bless ye! don't I know the lek?
And the little shiver, and wrappin the neck,
And lookin at the moon and sigh'n,
And whisp'rin—aw the Ballaquine
Wasn the only place, d'ye hear—
Not it! not it! aw dear! aw dear!
Strainin out through honeysuckles,
Or ivy, and her hair in buckles
Of coils and coils; and her body stretchin
Lek far away, lek longin, lek retchin
To heaven itself, lek tuk and caught
At[1] some angel—and even you forgot—

[1] By.

Yis, and then a sniff and a sniggle,

And just the smallest taste of a giggle

Lek—bless my sowl! you'd think it was sporras

In the thatch beginnin their little good-morrows.

And then the coolin of the mornin air,

And things goin a seein everywhere,

And the crow of the cock, and the stir of the cows,

And the dead white light on the front of the house—

Aw they do'n' like that! aw no they do'n'!

Aw bless ye! it's just about time to be go'n'

Then; but still you'll not be off

Till she shuts the window; and often enough

It'll be broad day in the garden there,

And she'll see you, if you can't see her.

So mind you'll be smart—d' ye hear me, you sir?

Just take my word—it'll be well to do ser.[1]

Aye, and this Nessy had a way

That lots of them has, to take and stay

A bit behind a curtain or that—

Aw, bless your life! just a bit of a cat

---

[1] So.

In the whole of them—aw, I'll allow—
Lek seein how are ye actin now.
You think her eye isn on you—take care!
They're rather dangerous, they are,
That way—aye—bein it's mornin—
And just, ye know, to see if you're yawnin,
Or the lek o' that; and 'scusable
If you are, you know; but they navar will,
No, not them—no use! no use of ye!
Bless ye! they'll navar take excuse of ye!
Navar! navar! and all the same
You don't want to be slopin—it's just like a dhrame;
You're greedy of any chance she might come
Back to the window—the way with some—
Back, and back. And you're still as death,
And the honeysuckles seems full of her breath—
And—yes, it is! and—no, it is'n!
She's gone! she's gone! and the sun is risen.
There, there! I couldn help it, my men—
Aisy then! aisy then!

Well that was Jack and Harry's style,
And lek enough the best of a mile

To the farm, but takin differin ways

Reggilar; and Jack 'd ha' crase [1]

Mostly of Harry, but couldn hinder

But the two of them meetin under the winder.

Jack fuss, and Harry to folla—

And Harry more like a dooiney-molla [2]

For Jack, lek helpin him to woo,

But takin his turn at the winder too—

Aw honour bright! but not much, ye see,

To say for himself, this Henery—

Not him—and puzzled, I doubt,

Puzzled enough to hould out

The time that Jack was givin him—shy,

And *hum and hem*, and "Aye, woman? aye?"

That was the most she got out of Harry—

Aw, a dacent chap! aw varry! varry!

But 'lowanced of brain—that's it! that's it!

'Lowanced enough, and navar fit

For the likes of her, that could dance all round him

With the tongue, and altogether confound him—

And—"Aye, woman? aye?" till at last she says—

---

[1] Would have the start.

[2] Man-praiser, the friend who backs, and speaks praisingly of the suitor.

" It's no use o' churnin away like this,

And navar no butter."   And—" Come ! will ye talk

About Jack ?" she says, and he wouldn baulk

The young woman of coorse.   " Very well," says he,

And on about Jack, and fiddlededee—

And what did he think of Jack ? was he right

In his mind, did he think ? and rather a flight

Of a craythur—what ? and no doubt takin care—

The way she was spakin—that Jack would hear—

And Jack nearly choked with the rage—good Lord,

But bitendin not to hear a word.

    And then she'd make her note that sweet

And soft and trimblin—it was like the tweet

Of a young duck.   And - *Wasn he nice*

This Jack ?—aw dear ! and couldn he tice

The arm off a gel ?   And — *Wasn he a love ?*

And *wasn he a darlin ?*   and a surt of a shove

With the words, like arrars [1] from the quivers,

Sendin Jack in the fits of shivers.

    And couldn stand it, poor fellow, of coorse,

---

[1] Arrows.

And rushin on Harry, and as hoorse as hoorse,

And whisp'rin, " Look here ! the time is up."

Then says Nessy, " Suppose I want him to stop—

Time, indeed ! whose time ? bad 'cess !

You're thinkin a dale of yourself," she says,

" It's for me, not for you, to tell him to go—

Time did ye say ? But I'll have you to know."

And stoops—and—" Listen, Harry, will ye ?

I've got something partikkilar to tell ye.

Jack musn hear. Be off with ye, Jack,

To the apple-tree, and don't come back

Till I tell ye." The apple-tree—that was the place

They had to stand, in any case,

When their coortin was off, just like it would be

Their watch on deck—aye—the apple-tree——

> " Apple-tree, apple-tree,
>   Cover me, cover me,
>   Branches of the apple-tree !
>   While night's shadows drift and flee,
>   Fall on me, fall on me,
>   Blossoms of the apple-tree—
>   Pink-tipt snowflakes tenderly
>   Gliding from the apple-tree !"

Aye, them's Tommy's, Tommy Big-eyses [1]—

[1] See *Fo'c's'le Yarns.*

Terble for rimin—all surts and sizes,
Tommy, bless ye!

             But Brew, the father—
It's lek you're thinkin it curious rather
He was navar hearin them at these games.
Well, lizzen to me ; that man was the same's
A pig for the sleepin and the snorin—
See-saw ! Margery Daw !
Roarin, borin—
No starts, no snarts arrim [1]—studdy he done it,
Studdy directly he begun it—
Say about half-past-eight or that
Till maybe four in the mornin—chat ! [2]
Yandhar man ! you could hear pretty farrish
The snore of him—fit to shake the parish.

    So of coorse.   But lek enough you'll be sayin
Boosely music to be playin
Lek a surt of accomplamink
To the coortin - and aisy so to think,
Aisy, natheral ; but still
People that's coortin, ye see, they will ;

    [1] At him, on his part.   [2] Chut, tut.

And somethin to know the ould chap's safe—

I'd rather trust him snorin than deaf,

'Deed I would.   But you wouldn sundher

From the gel you love for the roots of thundher.

But couldn help laughin sometimes—pirry us ![1]

Special Harry, that wasn that sirrious,[2]

Nor that deep like Jack : but often corrected

At this fellow —*Her father must be respected*

To his very snore, says Jack, as sollum

As avar ye seen a what-d'ye-call-um.

And had they it all to themselves that tune ?

What was all the other chaps doin ?

Well, you'll observe, it wasn none

But the miner lads that ever done

The reg'lar sooreyin that's in,[3]

Lek what they're callin sooreyin—

Proper lek—you know the surt—

Them other chaps I was tellin, that dirt

Of shoemakers, and tailors, and jiners

And that, was freckened [4] of the miners,

---

[1] Pity us, good gracious !   [2] Serious.

[3] Courting that *is* courting.   [4] Frightened.

Reg'lar freckened, and navar dar'd
Show a nose inside of the yard
After the milkin—no—they dar'n'—
Aw they're not to be trifled with, miners ar'n'—
You'd batthar belave it ! one or two of them
Tried it a bit, but all the crew of them
Jined—these miners down at the Pub,
Members of the " Nessy Club "—
Yis, that's what they were callin the 'ciety—
And they tuk such urdher,[1] and worked such variety
Of ghoses and goblins, and big bogganes,[2]
Like divils growlin in their dens,
And groanin terble behind the fences,
That they freckened these fellas urrov[3] their senses.

So that was all right ; and Harry and Jack
Had no more trouble with the lek.
But every one their own troughs—
That was the coortin of these boughs[4]—
Boughs, ye know   yis, that was the name—
Pushin each other—a rum surt o' game

[1] Order, made such arrangements.
[2] The " lubber fiend " of Milton.
[3] Out of.   [4] Poor (creatures).

To plase a gel ; and laughin that rough—
A passil o' donkeys, sure enough !

But still these two had another plan—
Jack, of coorse, the head man,
And Harry was willin either way ;
But Jack persuaded him to lay
The thing before the cõmmĭtteē
Of the club, and—*Couldn they all agree*
That Jack and Harry had the chance,
And let the others go to France,
Or Jericho? And statin their case—
And "for-as-much," and "the year of grace "—
And signed and sealed, and *made declar*[1]
That Nessy was favourin them far
Above the other chaps ; and so
What was the good for them to go
Any more ? and the register at them[2]
To stop at once, and just to let them
Settle it theirselves, whichever
Nessy'd chice,[3] *and for him to have her*—
Aw, as true as I'm a sinner—

---

[1] Declaration.   [2] Their register.   [3] Chose.

And fair play, and back the winner!

And tuk their davies,[1] bein as't,[2]

And proposed and seconded, and passed

Umnanermous [3]—and " Do-to-wit," [4]

And " Amen," and " So be it"!

Very sollum—makin motions—

Aw, these miners has their notions.

From that very day there wasn a sowl

Interferin ; but Jack got foul

Of these tailor-lads and all the rout,

And he wouldn have them comin about.

And he went to Brew, and he axed him to act –

" It's puffeck " scandalous," says Jack,

" Puffeck scandalous."   " And you,

What are you after then?" says Brew

" Aye, man, aye? if I may make so bould."

So Jack bucked up to him, and tould

All about it.   And—" Bless my life !

And is she goin to be your wife ?

Yours?" says Brew, "engaged, it's lek ?

---

[1] Affidavits.   [2] A ked.   [3] Unanimously.

[4] Fragment of diplomatic phrace.   [5] Perfectly.

Engaged is it? a purty speck!"[1]

"No," says Jack, " but goin to be—

Coortin."—" Coortin ! fiddlededee !

Botheration ! what d'ye say?

You're coortin reg'lar?   Coort away !

But these collaghs[2] that's comin about the farm

Of an evenin—bless my sowl !   What harm ?

Rather company, lek a surt of a cheerin."

    But Jack was terble perseverin—

"They're jokin her," he says, " and provokin her," he says,

" Till she up's and at them out and in,

And gives them the imperince of sin—

And isn nathral in her—no !

And it's spilin the gel ; and it's boosely show !"[3]

And she isn nice that way a bit,

And it isn right, and it isn fit ;

And you've got the torrity,[4] Masthar Brew,

So give them it ! aw do, aw do !"

"Torrity," says Brew, " gallivantin !

I'll torrity them, if it's that what you're wantin."

---

[1] A pretty speculation.   [2] Lads.

[3] Very beastly, very bad.   [4] Authority.

"Torrity!" and as grim as grim—
So this was the way he torritied them.

The very next evenin—aw navar fail!
He come upon the street with a flail—
'Clear out of this!" says he, and a slash
Lek every way—"clear out, ye trash!
Clear out!" he says, "ye Skilligalee!
These wayses isn shuitin me—
Clear out!" and he made another quiver,
And they cleared that yard pretty quick, however.
Aw yis, I tell ye—and Nessy that white
With the mad, and standin on her right,
And— "Nice work!" and wouldn speak
To the father or Jack the best of a week.

But coaxed, did Jack, aw coaxed her though,
And Harry to help him, and the orchard like snow
That year up yandhar, like snow: you'd see't
The best of a mile- aw a reg'lar sheet—
Most beautiful.   And Lord love ye!
The nice it is to have yandhar above you
And all around you, as you may say
Apple-blossom in the middle of May.

That's the coortin! Aw, lave it alone!

The Queen of England upon her throne

Might envy you then. The trees like nets

All knotted over with white rosettes,

Like white ladies standin theer—

In the spring—of coorse: in the fall of the year

I don't know; but still, for a chice—

But bless ye! an orchard is allis nice:

It's like heaven, I think, and the angels flittin

From tree to tree, and you to be sittin

With . . . well, well, well! the Lord can save,

The Lord, the Lord it was that gave,

Gave her, gave her, and tuk her the same,

And blessed be His holy name!

Aisy, lads! it's a finish night—

All right, all right!

So, as I was a-sayin—aye, aye, in the fall

Maybe not so nice; but still the smell

Of the apples—aw dear! they'll do ye! they'll do ye!

Aw through and through ye! through and through
        ye!

It's a very lovin smell is apples—

This stuff the Romans burns in their chapels
Is very sweet ! but what is it comparin
To apples, special goin a-bearin
In an orchard--all a surt of 'spicion
Of rum things about, like some faery was fishin
With a smell for a bait—invisible—
Aw sartinly—but a smell, a smell.

And sure enough the sarpint knew't
'Deed he did, the ugly brute—
There's no mistake it's that that done
Eve altogether—— I mean, begun,
For ate she did, and so did Adam,
But ate she needn -this tasty madam,
No—but smellin she couldn help
That's where he had her   this divil's whelp,
Had her for sure.
        But what a place
That garden must have been ! bad 'cess
To them that lost it for us - aye !
And let them boo, and let them cry,
Had to turn out that very minute—
A garden ' Why, God was walkin in it

In the cool of the day, the Bible's tellin—

Dear me! the grand it must ha' been smellin!

Talk of gardens! talk of loss!

But what a donkey that Adam was

Hidin himself aback o' the bushes,

Him and Eve, like a pair of big thrushes,

And only—but bless me! the foolishness!

But loss [1] the place! loss the place!

The garden, aye! the garden of Eden—

But an orchard too—the way we're readin

About yandhar fruit, and the terble desi'ble [2]

For food and that, but scandlus li'ble

To die if you eat.   But the Ballaquine

Had a orchard—aw dear! but—never mind!

There's no doubt but God Himself might ha' walked

In yandhar place, and heard what was talked.

Sooreyin? [3] yes, sooreyin!

I'll tell ye what it is, my men—

You don't understand—this gel was gud,

And so was Jack: there's love that's mud,

---

[1] Lost.   [2] Desirable.   [3] Courting.

Not love—I know, I know, Bill Mat,
Ah! no need to tell me o' that!
But love that 'll take a gel, and liff her
To the heaven of heavens, that's the differ;
No black disgrace, but pure, man, pure
As the sthrames that gathers in old Ballure—
Why wouldn God be with the lek?
Walkin, list'nin, I expeck,
Aye, and blessin—fruits and flowers,
What are they all to the hearts that pours
All their joy and all their love
Into one another? God above!
An honest gel and an honest lad!
Can Thou see them, and not be glad?
Thou sees, Thou knows, Thou loves them aye!
Every kiss and every sigh,
Every sigh and every kiss,
Even if it's not in Genesis.

Be happy then, my lovin birds!
God bless true sweethearts! them's the words—
A holier thing, and no mistake in,[1]

[1] There is no mistake.

He navar made in all His makin—
True as steel—but don't forget,
God's walkin in the garden yet !

Queer soorcyin ? you're thinkin, eh ?
Well that depends, as one may say,
On who you are, and what you are—
Of coorse ! of coorse ! my man-o'-war !
There's sarpints in the garden too,
Aw, as common as *how-d'ye-do !*
Yis ! and howavar the happy you'll be,
It's well to remember Him that can see
Your very heart, and if it's clane,
He'll make you twice as happy again.

Terble religious I got on the sudden ?
Jemmy, ate your own pudden,
Do now, do ! it'd be a dale batter ;
You don't know much about the matter,
Not much, I think.   There was used to be once
A thing they was callin innocence—
Now then, Jemmy !   It's God that picks them,
These lovers, and He stands betwix them ;

Every look, and every breath
Is God's ; they're faithful unto death,
Because God is faithful ; not thinkin of Him,
Lek enough, but Him of them
Sartin sure.   No saint wasn Jack,
Nor Nessy ither, lek you'll see in a track—
No ! but only the nither 'd ha' seen
The other in trouble for the wealth of the Queen ;
And if it had happened, I'll tell ye what—
Jack 'd ha' cut his throat like a shot,
And Nessy's too—bless ye ! outragers !
Hot as fire ! so that's the relajers ![1]

Yes, and still this Nessy was tazin him
Despard though, aw nearly crazin him—
And touch-me-not ! and sniffs and snuffs,
And sulks and sulks, and huffs and huffs.
And was the Lord betwix them then ?
Aisy ! with them ? with them, my men ?
With them ? with them ? . . . and what for wouldn He ?
With them ! with them ! and what for shouldn He ?
With them ! with them !   sartinly !

The religious.

And d—— it all! don't talk to me!

D'ye hear?

But lizzen now what will folla—

This Harry was chiced[1] for a dooiney-molla,

Chiced complate; and went with Jack

Every night—aw he wouldn be slack!

Givin up all notion of Nessy,

Aw, aisy-goin urrov messy![2]

And made up his mind it wasn no use,

And dooiney-mollain like the deuce.

Fuss-rate—ye see the chap

Wasn worth the smallest scrap

At lovin, no! it was dooiney-mollain

That he was good for, follain, follain,[3]

Buckin up, lek what you'd call a—

Well, you know—— a dooiney-molla—

That's it—lek semperthizin

Pirriful[4]—aw quite surprisin—

Yis—lek lovin just to be theer,

Just to lizzen—this Harry Creer—

---

[1] Chosen. [2] Out of mercy, extraordinarily. [3] Following.
[4] Pitifully, wonderfully.

Aye, and, every kiss that was go'n,
Just to give a little moan
Urrov[1] him, very low and soft,
Or maybe a little bit of a cough
Or the lek ; but keepin as close as close,
That he wouldn be missin the smallest ghost
Of a sound or a sigh, and laenin his chin
On Jack's shouldher, and lizzenin.
Lizzenin—and his breath goin pourin
Agen[2] Jack's ear, and had to be cowrin
Rather—stoopin, ye know, for the big
He was compared to Jack ; and 'd twig
Every little hitch that was clickin,
And Jack's heart that was goin a-tickin
Like a clock. And Nessy up in the windher,
But none so high ; and Jack to meandher
Some dodge to get nearer, to hould her hand
When she'd stretch it down, you'll understand.

And sometimes he'd get a'top of a tub,
Or anything that was handy, a scrub
Of a trammon[3] that was growin there

---

[1] Out of.   [2] Against.   [3] Elder-tree.

Aw, lave him alone! aw, navar fear!

Bless ye! he was soople was Jack;

And sometimes gettin on Harry's back,

And standin on Harry's shouldher, and flingin

His arms round Nessy's neck, and bringin

Her face to his in the very middle

Of the honeysuckles—aw then the thriddle

Of thrimblin that shivered the back of this Harry—

Semperthizin—bless ye! very—

Semperthizin—didn I say?

Semperthizin anyway.

"Get down!" says Nessy, "don't ye see

That Harry is tired?"—"Not me! not me!"

And just like a mason with his hod,

As stiff—and beggin for the love of God

They'd go on; and gevvin[1] a surt of a coo—

"Aw keep it up! aw do! aw do!"

And as strong as a bull, and wouldn be beat.

But sweethearts can't be allis like that,

With a fellow to lizzen to all they're say'n—

Bless your sowl! the thing is plain—

Can't: so sometimes Harry had orders

---

[1] Giving.

F

To stand a bit off aback o' some borders.

Or under the biggest apple-tree.

So there this dooiney-molla 'd be,

Very patient, but strainin, strainin

To hear the coortin, and lek enough rainin,

Or snowin, or blowin—

Dear me! what's the odds?   No knowin

The happy Harry was, just to be catchin

The smallest whisper; like a hen when she's hatchin.

Sittin that quite;[1] but the little sweep

Is liz'nin too for some sign of a cheep

At[2] one of the eggs—aw deed she is.

And so this Harry; and if he heard a kiss,

Which of coorse he did, and raisonable,

He'd moan the softest he was able—

Like a flute he'd moan, like a flute! surprisin!

Semperthizin, semperthizin.

So—very well! very well!

Aye—but now I've got somethin to tell,

That you'll maybe be wondhrin the change, d'ye hear!

The change that come on Harry Creer.

---

[1] Quietly.   [2] On the part of.

The aunt—the aunt; aye! that's the woman—

Misthriss Banks, and hemmin and hummin,

And hintin—— but wait a bit—— a wedda [1]

She was, and lived above the medda [2]

At the Ballaquine—a kind of a 'cess [3]

Up there, bein rather a boosely [4] place;

And the house like these sheds where the herrins is saltin

At Derby Haven—a reg'lar thalthin! [5]

Herself and her son was livin there,

But how she was livin—— well, I'll swear

I don't know, and still I do.

Ye see, he was an aisy man, was Brew;

But he wouldn have her in the house,

No he wouldn; and the wuss [6] of his cows

He gave her—and just a bit of a crof'

T'other side of the gill that was wallin off

From the farm, lek separate, more of a Lhergy [7]

Than anything else. And a chap called Curghey

Was jinin next to her—*Curphey*—says Jem—

Curghey and Curphey's all the same—

---

[1] Widow.　　[2] Meadow.　　[3] Recess, nook.　　[4] Beastly, rough.

[5] Half-ruined cottage.　　　　[6] Worst.

[7] High waste-land.

Miser'ble land, hafe[1] rock, hafe feerins,[2]

And the rest of it cushags,[3] and havin its bearins

Nor'-west of the Ballaquine. But she didn

Live on her land, let alone her midden,

Nor the cow ; for the cow was starvin with her,

And the croft it navar got nothin ither,

No care, nor 'tintion : not much for work

Wasn Misthriss Banks. If she'd had the Perk[4]

Of Barrule—*Llewellyn's?* to be sure !

Owned at[5] William Fyne Moor—

She'd ha' been just the same. So how then, how

Was the woman livin ? Don't make a row !

I'll tell ye ; the woman was livin on a pension

From a sartin party we'd best not mention—

She done his work, and she earned his wages,

Aw, that's the terms the ould chap engages——

He's got his grip o' them—touch for touch

A wutch ?[6] Of coorse she was a wutch,

And a black wutch, the wuss that's goin -

The white is   - well, I'm hardly knowin

Is the lek in :[7] but these ould things

---

[1] Half.   [2] Ferns.   [3] Ragwort.   [4] Park, large enclosure.

[5] By.   [6] Witch.   [7] Do such exist.

That's sellin charms to sailors, rings,

Papers, ye know—why, bless my sowl !

Here's one at me [1]—it's middlin oul',

Wore I don't know the teens of years

On my heart here, look, la !   Sally Tear's

The woman that sould it—in Castletown—

Queen Street—aye—and half-a-crown . . .

I spose the most of ye's got the lek

Somewhere hung around your neck.

   But there's odds of charms ; for some is just

A surt of a blessin ; but some is a cuss,

Most bitther, brewed in the very gall

Of spite and hate, and 'll creep and crawl

Over your body and over your sowl,

Aye, man ! aye ! at laste so I'm tould—

And through and through, and makin you sick,

And makin you mad—aw, they know the trick !

Cussin your fingers and cussin your toes,

Cussin your mouth and cussin your nose,

Every odd jint, and every limb,

And all your inside—that's the thrim—

---

[1] In my possession.

Cussin your horse and cussin your cow,

Cussin the boar and cussin the sow—

Everything that's got a tail ;

Aye, and your spade, and your cart, and your flail,

Plough and harras,[1] stock and crop,

Nets and lines—they'll navar stop—

Treminjis cussin—*charms?* yis !

But writin   no ! but spit and hiss

And mutter and mumble—that's your surt !

Rags that's tore from the divil's ould shirt —

He'll claim his own.   You'll be passin by,

And not a word, but the evil eye—

There ye are ! you're struck, they've done ye !

They've got ye—you're tuck ! they've put it upon ye —

Aw boosely shockin !   And harbs ! they picks them

The right time of the moon, and they'll take and mix
        them—

I've seen this woman myself goin pryin

Under the hedges, and stoopin and spyin ;

And if she seen me, she'd give a gurn

Most horrid at me.   Yis, and they'll burn,

And they'll fry and they'll stew, and makin faces

[1] Harrows.

What is it they won't do?—Brutes o' bases!

I know their par and I know their mar—

Divils! divils! that's what they are!

And should be tuk and burnt the way

They used to be—by gough, I'll lay

You'd smell the brimstone—you would so—

But no justice now, nor nothin—no!

Terble changes—takin and slammin them

In the Lunertic Asylum—crammin them

With the best o' good livin, and rates and taxes,

And a doctor, and anything they axes—

At the Sthrang[1] there—aye! and a mortal buildin,

And the money flyin, and carvin and gildin,

And a fine sittervation, terble airy——

And hip-hooraa for Robby Fairy![2]

" Down with the taxes!" says Robby, "bad luck with
  them!"

Taxes! aw Robby 'll have no truck with them.

But the 'sylum wasn thought of then;

And she wasn threescore years and ten,

---

[1] The Isle of Man Lunatic Asylum at the Strang, near Douglas.

[2] Famed as a nondescript reformer.

Wasn Misthriss Banks, nor sixty ither,

But 'stonishin the way they'll wither—

The lek—aw a reg'lar flibberty-gibberty

Surt of a woman, and liked her liberty,

Aye, and tuk it.   And when she was drest

And titervated all in her best,

And her white stockin, and her lastin slipper,

I tell ye she looked a reg'lar clipper,

Tasty uncommon at Hollantide fair

Or the lek—aw the tastiest woman there—

Painted, ye know —aw lips and cheeks,

Like plaster just, lek goin in streaks,

Like varnish mostly, like polish, like size ;

And I don't know what the divil she was doin to her

    eyes—

Like a play-acthur.   So with all this criss-crosserin,[1]

And dabbin and grainin[2] and pink-saucerin,[3]

You'd hardly thought, of the whole bilin,

You got the blackest wutch on the Islan.

    But still we hev it in Revelation

And about the *cup of abomination* -

---

[1] Some vague idea of hatching (shading) seems meant.
[2] In painting.   [3] A primitive dye, or cosmetic.

And—*the blood of the saints*—— and goin a-dressin

In a scarlet frock, like a foreign pessin—

A bad lot that—— and Jezebel,

Lookin out at the windher—aw a despard swell!

And *painted her face, and tired her head*—

" Fling her down !" this Jehu said—

" Fling her down !" and tuk and swung her—

One—two—" Fling !" aw by gough they flung her.

Aw Jehu was mortal boosely though—

You mind the heads there all in a row,

Seventy of them at the gate,

And kings' sons, and lekly as nate

As a pin, and the hair of them just like silk,

And comin in in the mornin with the milk—

Aw Jehu—— well, I havn a word

To say—but still—— ye see, the Lord—

So lave it alone ; but, of a rule,

Them ould kings was middlin cru'l.

Misthriss Banks ! Misthriss Banks !

Aw, a big long woman, thin in the flanks,

That, when she was up to these divil's pranks,

It had ha' took Ould Harry himself to hould her—

High in the hips, and high in the shoulder—

Yes, and I was tellin just now

The stunnin she looked, and the when and the how,

And round the Cape, and past Bigode.

And cock her up! and clear the road!

And in on the fair—*The Hills?*[1] eh, what?

Sartinly! the ould spot.

And rings and rings, and silk and satin,

Aw as grand as grand! and goin a-traitin[2]

At[3] the lads, of coorse. But the evenin

Was another pair of oars, my men.

Screwed? is it *screwed?* dead drunk, if ye plaze,

Like a bustin tar-barrel all in a blaze

Of cussin and blastin, and laughin and cryin

And singin —aw, if you'd only ha' heard her!

And a splash and a mash, and kickin and lyin

In a surt of a midden of muck and murder!

Foamin, frothin, splitter-splutter,

Like fits, like possessed aw roult in the gutter;

Somethin lek it's put in the Acts—

I don't azackly remember the facts,

---

[1] The old Douglas fair-ground, on the estate known as "The Hills."

[2] Being treated.   [3] By.

But a woman that shouted, and lek enough whopt to 't
At[1] the scamps that kep her; but Paul put a stop to 't.

Not much of a 'sample for Nessy, you'll say—
Well, hardly, hardly anyway.
So that's the raison Brew wouldn hev her
In the house arrim theer,[2] and tuk and gev her
The thalthan—wouldn hev her, no!
Wouldn! wouldn! wouldn though!

Did I tell you about the chile she had?
Job he was callin—a lump of a lad
Them times, but younger till his cousin.
Short was Job—of his body he wasn;
But short of wit—the innercent
Ye navar—that's the way I meant—
Soft, no doubt, aw soft; but grew
A splandid falla; soft, but true
As steel, and gud, and full of grace,
And a beautiful face! a beautiful face!
Aw the gentle! aw the sweet!
I tell ye what—you wouldn meet
The lek of Job on a long day's march—

---

[1] Whipped to it by.   [2] With him there.

No you wouldn—and as straight as a larch—

Lovely made—and the big blue eye,

Aw fit to make a body cry!

And grew——— but that was years and years

Afterwards——— avast these tears—

Look at me!—another night

I'll give you Job——— all right! all right'

Aw a terble story--— but he wears the robe—

Washed, ah washed! poor Job! poor Job!

But the nither Job nor the mother was gettin

Admission to Brew's, except she'd be lettin

In at [1] Nessy on the sly,

When Brew was in bed—aw, she wouldn be shy

Wouldn yandhar; but freckened enough

Of Brew that cud be despard rough,

For all the aisy; but freckened though,

Freckened himself—aw, I'd have ye to know!

Freckened thallure;[2] for he knew she could wither

The heart of him into ould shoe-leather,

Or any other divilment—

Witchin, wutchin, wherever she went.

Wutchin sartin ; but kep it off

With this thalthan, and the cow, and the crof—

He had her there, and middlin safe,

He was thinkin—aye, but didn hafe [1]

Like the thing ; and made up his mind

She shouldn get in on the Ballaquine,

Her nor her child.

But the woman was fond

Uncommon of Nessy—or was it the bond,

And Nessy in it ; unknownst, of coorse,

To herself? but anyway such a foorce

She done of charms there, early and late,

That she put the comedher [2] on Nessy complate,

Clane [3] comedher, harpooned, and haulin it—

Fascernation the Pazon was callin it—

Fascernation—and might have been—

" Kayar ! [4] kayar ! " says ould M'Queen,

" That'll bring her up "—and maybe it will :

Tremenjers though, aw terrible !

Kayar, for the strong it was houldin the gel,

And spun from nothin but the wind of hell— .

That's the Kayar ! and wasn it a pity ?

---

[1] Half.   [2] Spell of attraction.   [3] Downright.   [4] Strong rope.

Poor thing ! the sweet and the pretty,

And the lovin too, and a d- — ould cat

To have her in her power like that !

So she tuk a notion of a surt of suppoortin

Nessy, like a shuperintendin the coortin,

Lek backin, lek watchin, lek a kind of encouragin ;

And waitin till dark, and goin a furragin

About the house ; and creep and creep—

And aisy to tell if Brew was asleep

With the snorin, bless ye !　And　"Come in ! come in !"

And whisperin and whisperin ;

And a bit of supper : and then Nessy 'd say

"Time for bed "　and—" Let me stay !

Aw let me ! let me !"　*And only right—*

And her aunt and all—and "Good-night ! good-night !"

At[1] Nessy.　Aw then she'd dart in her ear

Most despard cusses—navar fear !

And tellin the charms she had on Jack

She could turn ev'ry bit of his body black

She could make him hate her—poor Nessy Brew !

Nothin she couldn and wouldn do !

<hr />

[1] Said by.

And the gel, you know, as freckened as freckened,

Because of coorse she navar reckoned

But Misthriss Banks could do the jeel [1]

She was braggin she could, and she'd take and kneel

On her bended knees, and she'd cuss—the baste !

Cuss the very skin off your face—

But low, very low, that Brew wouldn wake—

A surt of a spittin like this new kind of brake

They've got on the railways—*air brake*, is it ?

The dirty thing, goin fizzit ! fizzit !

And spittin there.   So up to the room !

She should ha' been cocked on a lump of a broom

Sky-high—the ould Turk !

And then the comedher 'd begin to work ;

And she'd coax, and she'd clapse, and she'd play the deuce,

Till the poor thing was gettin all a confuse, [2]

Lek foolish lek ; and she'd kiss and she'd cuddle,

Till Nessy's head 'd be all in a muddle—

Swimmin lek, lek heavy—aye !

And when Jack 'd appear, poor Nessy 'd sigh,

And come to the window.   But the wutch 'd be lookin

Over her shouldher—and crouchin and crookin—

[1] Damage.   [2] In a state of confusion.

All eyes and ears—but the hitch on the tongue,
Lek the ould moon keekin behind the young,
You know—and the little thing middlin shy
To step out there in the big broad sky
Before all the stars—like a panerrammer,
Mostly. But the ould one—damn her!
She's up to no good that ever I knew,
At least for the likes of me and you.

But—wutches in front, dooiney-mollas aback -
What surt of coortin was that for Jack?
No coortin at all. And bore it wanst,
And bore it twicet; and then he danced
With ragin fury—*Such dirt goin muckin*
About the gel, he said, *and suckin*,
Yes, he said, *suckin her blood*,
Like a spider a fly, or makin crud[1]
Of it altogether; and where would it stop?
Drainin her heart to the last drop—
Quite aisy to see—the gel gettin white
Most pitiful—a reg'lar blight
On the gel, he said. He could *feel her drawin*

---

[1] Curd.

Back and back, lek some divil was clawin

And pullin her theer, and furder and furder,

Lek innards someway, lek some hole of murder

They were haulin her into : yis, and lavin

Just a shape, lek a surt of a graven

Image of Nessy at the windher,

And herself goin burnin into tindher,

In some place at [1] *these divils—aye tuk and hove her*

In a pit, and roullin her over and over

On coals of fire—and hotter and hotter—

Yis, yis, yis—and where had they got her?

That wasn Nessy—and he'd hev his revenge

And he'd stop this work, and this wutch should senge

In the deepest of hell herself. And he spoke

Middlin plain ; and *it wasn no joke*

For him, he said, *nor for Nessy,* he said :

And—" Go home with ye ! go ! go home to bed !

Who's wantin ye here—with your skinny throat?

You're a big black wutch, and I'd have ye to know't."

So the Banks to go and Jack to stay.

But the coortin was bruk at them anyway,

---

[1] By.

That night at least : for the aunt was gone
Like whisked through the keyhole : but Nessy was done,
Done complate, and trimblin theer
Most awful.   And- " Darlin !" and " Navar fear !"
At¹ Jack ; but no use, and tuk and crept
Back in her bed, but never slept,
And worked at ² this wutch like the say is workin
With a tidesway, and all her body jerkin
And tossin like a fever ; and *oh !*
What would she do ?   And *she'd go, she'd go*
First thing in the mornin, she muss ! she muss !
And coax her that she wouldn cuss
This Jack.   But still the gel was fearin
The cuss 'd be done afore daylight appearin—
Burnin somethin, or raisin the divil,
Or God knows what.   And *why wasn he civil ?*
Civil, just civil !   Aw Jack then ! Jack then !
The pity !   And — *Would she call him back then ?*
Back ! back ! back !   And jumps to the windher—
But Jack was gone.   " He'll be burned to a cindher,"
Says Nessy - poor sowl !   You see, she knew
The despard things these wutches can do

¹ Said by.   ² By.

On all your body—aw horrid they can !

Horrid, I tell ye.   But that was the plan,

For Jack was for bustin in the door,

No matter whether Brew to snore

Or not to snore.   "Who knows if she's dyin ? "

And even to think of her theer a-lyin !

God bless him !   And he made a run, but caught

At[1] Harry straight, that said he thought

They'd better make haste, you know, and give sheet[2]

After this wutch.   And over the street,

And over the hedges and over the ditches,

And away for the Gill, but Harry got stitches

In his side or the lek, and puffin and pantin,

And couldn hould on, and began a slantin

For the road, bein middlin freckened she'd come

In some shape or another, like a corpse, by gum !

Or a modda-doo,[3] goin bawwawin,

Or a tarroo-ushtey,[4] or a muck-awin,[5]

Or—"Stop !" he says, "aw stop then ! stop ! "

And—*Bless his sowl ! he was like to drop ;*

And a cow gave a cough—aw Harry roared,

---

[1] By.   [2] Chase.   [3] Black dog (see *Peveril of the Peak*).

[4] Water-bull (fabulous).   [5] River-pig (fabulous).

And Harry screeched, and Harry implored,
And Jack that bothered he had to give in ;
And the two of them home with a safe skin
To Harry's lodgin, and slept together.
But beat, and feelin foolish rather.

The day was hardly bruk when Nessy
Was up to the Gill, and beggin for messy,[1]
And *for all the sakes!* and what she would give her :
And *couldn they be as thick as ever?*
And *Jack was onpatient, but Jack was gud :*
And she'd give her anything! yes, she wud!
She'd give her her brooch and her beautiful pin,
And her clasp, and the rael gool sovereign
She got in her box, and a velvet belt
That was speckled with flowers, and the buckle gilt
Most lovely—aye ! poor thing ! poor thing !
And ribbons and scarfs!   " Will you give me the ring
You've got on your finger then ? " says the aunt -
Her mother's weddin ring she meant -
" Will you give me that ? "   Then Nessy shook
All over, and she gave a look

[1] Mercy.

At the woman, and aw, the pitiful!

And then at the ring, and begun to pull,

And stopped, and pulled, and stopped again,

And the tears come pourin down like rain;

And she snuggled her hand agin her breast,

And kissed and kissed and kissed and kissed—

The ring, of coorse, and looks up at the aunt,

And just a whisper—"I can't! I can't!——

I seen him take it . . . take it," she said,

"From her finger . . . —and the straight in the bed . . .

And the could, auntie, the could! the could! . . ."

And the poor gel shivered.   But the aunt to rowl

Her eyes like wheels, and her body stretched

To the full of her height, and tuk and retched

All over the child, till she fell right down,

Like stiff, like dead—aw then I'll be bound

She had her up and in her lap,

And *hushee bowbabbied*,[1] and *on the tree-top*,[1]

In a minute—aye, and stooped lek to cover her,

And sthrooghin[2] her theer, and breathin over her

The wutches breath, and hummin charms

In her ear; and all the strain of her arms,

---

[1] Fragments of a cradle-song.   [2] Stroking.

And the warmth, and the squeeze, and the curl, and the ply
Of all her body, till Nessy to sigh,
And Nessy to move.   And then . . . and then . . .
She'd got another plan, my men.

    "Aw no!" she said, "well no then! no!
Aw not the ring! but . . . lizzen though!
Lizzen . . . the key of the ould man's chist"
(Her father) . . . "five pound wouldn be missed
Urrov[1] yandhar lot." . . . *Could she get the key?*
And . . . sometime he'd be out of the way . . .
What? Aw Nessy gave a spring,
And "Take it! take it! take the ring!
For God's sake! take it! take it! take it!
Here! here! will that do? will that make it
All right?" she says; "you'll not wutch him
Jack, you won't?"   "I'll never touch him,"
Says Mrs. Banks ; *and she'd come next night*
For the other things. So Nessy tuk flight
Like a partridge: and—"She driv[2] me! she driv me!"
And "Mother! mother! forgive me! forgive me!"
Poor Nessy! and all the way she was goin

---

        [1] Out of.   [2] Drove.

She was sighin and sobbin and makin her moan—
"This is love!" she said, "and the nice it'd be
If it wasn for the misery!"

And I'll tell ye what, the gel had raison,
She had, aw yes! for it's just amazin
The work that's with it.   But still for all
Who'd be without it? to stand or to fall,
The sweet with the bitter!   But the poor young things,
That's feelin love like birds feels wings,
And up's like the lark, and love to crown them
With joy, and the sun all round and round them—
And then comes hail and frost and snow,
And the thunders rowl, and the winds they blow—
Aw dear, the poor birds! *It's better, you'd think,*
To have nothin to do with it?   Chink-chink-chink!
Chunk-chunk-chunk![1]   Well, of coorse ye needn :
Bless ye! there's different sorts of feedin—
Pigs isn larks, not them ; and still
Pigs is very comfible—
Jine the pigs! it's the easiest way,
Shove your snout in the trough, and suck away!

---

[1] Imitates the sound of coin.

Now Nessy had ha' done much batthar
If she'd ha' come and tould the matthar
To me.   For I was young, that's true,
But still I was gran' for advisin : there's few
Could ha' beat me, no!   And of coorse I'd ha' gone
And tould the Pazon, and the thing had been done
At once—God bless ye! sartinly!
The Pazon! done? my goodness me!
But I suppose I *was* too young
For a gel like her to have took and brung
Her sorrow to—it was years and years.
After all her hopes and all her fears
Was settled lek, she was tellin me,
Aw, no mistake, and as free as free -
Tellin—bless ye! tellin uncommon -
Aw, I knew the woman ! I knew the woman !
Jack ? well . . . Jack . . . go tellin him ?
Not her! not her!   This despard limb
Was no good for advisin—lovin, yes—
But that's another sort of guess
Lovin   and dooiney-mollain too
Well, you see, it'd hardly do
It's not what they're for, being wanted to praise

A chap to his sweetheart—let them keep their place

These dooiney-mollas, not 'visin [1] *her*—

Lek I tould ye, eh? that's not what they're fur.

And as for Harry—Harry advisin?

Bless ye! Harry was stupid supprisin.

No, it was me—aw never fear!

But still it couldn be; so . . . theer!

And did she come down in the evenin

For the rest of the things?   Aye did she then,

And had them too, most sartinly,

And as good as money, and away on the spree

To Ramsey, and not a public-house

Goin or comin that this boosely throuss [2]

Didn have her dhrop.   So Crow,

That was drivin the coach, he found her though

Next mornin at King Orry's grave, [3]

Drunk as a fish, and tuk and gave

Her a tip with his whip, and waked her up—

Aw fond of a sup! fond of a sup!

But she kept her word though—curious!

[1] Advising.   [2] Slut.   [3] Near Laxdale.

Not the smallest taste of a cuss
Done on Jack, by night or by day :
But she worked the job another way —
'Deed she did though, worked it gran' —
Bless ye ! Harry was her man.
Sent for Harry to come and see her,
Which he went, but in terble fear,
Aw, mortal uncommon ! But "Come in !" she says,
"And a cup of tay ; and nice it is
To see a friend," and all to that [1] —
And Harry lookin hard at the cat,
And all about, and wondherin
Where was she keepin the rum and the gin,
And her dirts and her divilments *in crocks,*
Harry was thinkin, or — *was it a box ?*
Or bladders was it ? or under her clothes,
Or hid in the floor, or goodness knows !
Up the chimley lek enough,
And'd come to take him by the scruff,
All of a suddin, as black as ink
The divil aye didn know what to think.
But the place was swept, you know, and clane,

And the taypot singin, and pinjane [1]—
And the kettle you might have seen your face in't,
And everything as dacent as dacent—
Till Harry took heart, and eat like a melya,[2]
Made a very good tay, I tell ye.

And they talked of the croft, and they talked of the garden,
And they talked of her son, *that was only herdin*
Yet, she said ; *but she hoped he'd soon*
Have a job at the mines, and then he'd be do'n—
At an engine, perhaps, but hard to tell,
And the cows was shuitin him very well,
And away on the mountains mostly he was.
Herdin for Clague's of the Ballacross,
And only home at odds of time,
Just that Clague would take and try'm—
And a child, you know, and couldn expec',
And rather weak in his interlec',
But not so bad. "But, Harry Creer,
How is it there's some not far from here
That's got pluck and wit, and all the rest,
And handsome chaps, and a match for the best,

---

[1] Curds-and-whey.   [2] Feast at Harvest-home.

And still they don't see it?   Plenty of sanse
And everything . . . and don't see their chance,
Don't see it . . . but there's some that does,
Sees it plain does some of us."
And then she set upon him, and—*Who
Was this Jack Pentreath? and Nessy Brew!
Bless her sowl then! was he blind?
Nessy at the Ballaquine!
Nessy . . . cravin for him! Jack?
Nonsense! nonsense! just a pack
Of stuff and nonsense, a trick, a dodge
To get to be with Harry—fudge!
Make a fool of him?   No, she wudn,
But worshippin the ground he stood on.*

Aw she worked him well, till the chap was gapin
With his mouth like an oyster, the way she was shapin
The fool to her plan.   " By gough!" says Harry,
" I'll try it this night, and aisy—very—
To try—and *Sartinly! that's it!
Buck up! buck up a bit!*
And he'd soon see.   And *that little black imp
To be coortin Nessy! a surt of a shrimp*

Of a cockcroach coortin Nessy!   No!

And—*he-he-he!* and *ho-ho-ho!*

"It's you, Harry, idikkilis!

And the handsome ye are! and give me a kiss——·

There now, Harry! and spake to him, will ye!

Spake to him! spake to him, m'gilya!"[1]

   Poor Harry! aw kissed her fair and fit,

But wiped his mouth, and gave a spit

When he got outside, bein freckened, poor chap!

What pison'd come from the divil's trap

Of a mouth, that wasn a bad mouth ither—

Not ugly, I mean, but well-looked rather.

   So that night no wutch; but Nessy like chalk,

And Harry first goin up the walk;

And—"Wait!" he says to Jack, "just wait!

You see, I've been thinkin a dale of late,

And I don't know azackly, but still I'm wantin

To have a understandin or sonthin[2]—

A understandin—that's the tee,

A understandin is it you, is it me.

     [1] My lad.   [2] Something.

I'm not for no more dooiney-mollerin,
I've had enough of humbuggin and follerin ;
And I've raison to think—for I've heard at [1] them
That knows—that Nessy is . . . well . . . ahem . . .
Gettin rather fond—"   "Of you ?"
Says Jack ; "all right ! that'll do ! that'll do !"
And darts to the windher, and just a word
To Nessy, that maybe hardly heard
What was it he said, the treih [2] she was,
Poor thing ! and turns, and gives a toss
With his head.   "Now then," he says, "now then !
I've said good-night : down glen ! down glen !
This must be looked to."   And the fiery he spoke
Poor Harry seen it wasn no joke,
And had to go.   And directly they come
Upon the road—aw, sword and drum !
At it ! at it ! tongue, not fisses—
Jack's tongue mostly ; and "I insisses,"
Says Jack, "you'll 'splain the for and the how,
And what the deuce you're meanin—now,
Now," he says, "go on !"   But he didn
Wait for Harry.   "Turn up the midden !

----

[1] From.   [2] Sad.

Turn it up!" he says; but he turned

The midden up hisself. And he girned,

And he stamped, and he called him all the names

That ever was called. And —*Fire and flames!*

What was this? And —*Was he mad?*

Or what was he? Was it a divil he had?

Possessed? was that it? limb from limb!

Nessy gettin fond of him!

And —*Aw the fool!* and *aw the ungrateful!*

And —*Aw the donkey!* and *aw the decateful!*

And —*Aw the horrid!* and *aw the hateful!*

"Me that was lettin ye come spoortin

Under the shadder of my coortin!

Me that was lettin ye see the white

She was in the moon! and standin quite

Near, near! Didn I let ye?

And feelin her breath—and didn I set ye

To spake to her too? and what could ye spake?

And warn't ye hangin on my neck,

And her face agin mine, and smellin, smellin

Love's very flower, and hearin me tellin

The deepest saycrets of my heart?

And never to stir and never to start,

And never to make the smallest objection,

But *delighted*, ye said, *to see the affection*,

And the sweet soft coo there was in,[1] ye said,

It was music fit to wake the dead—

And never tired, and tit for tat,

And purrin there like a big tom-cat

The satisfied!   But now I see!

Is it you? or is it me?

Listen then, if you want to know!

It's me, you thund'rin lump of dough!

You ideit!" and on like crazy.

But Harry could only get in an "Aisy!"

Now and then—"Aisy!" he'd say,

"Aisy for all!" lek a sort of a way

To be hum'rin the chap.   And hotter and hotter!

Till Harry must ha' been made of botter,

Or porridge or somethin, if he could have bore

The jaw any longer.   And at last he swore

He wouldn stand it, and took and gript

This Jack, that ducked, and dipt, and slipt,

And quivered, and danced: but couldn hould him:

And Jack made a run for Harry, and bowled him

---

[1] *In* i pleona tic.

Over like a cock, and on to him,

And kep' him under, that was aisy done to him,

Bein heavy, and Jack like a bull pup,

And pinned him, and wouldn let him up

Till Harry would ax.   And then they stood

The two of them out of breath : and the blood

From Harry's nose, lek after an action

Two ships.   And " You'll give me satisfaction,"

Says Harry—" eh ? "   And—*the where and the when,*

And the how.   " At the mouth of the Dragon's den,"

Says Jack ; " let's see which 'll put the other

Down the ould pit, and finish this bother.

For you know d—— well whichever 'll lose

That bout," says Jack, " he'll have a long snooze

Down there, he will.   Now then, d'ye see !

It's death ! it's death 'twixt you and me !

Will you try the fall, my bloomin boss ?

Hands on it, Harry ! "   So it's hands it was.

The very next night no coortin in [1]—

No, and Nessy wondherin—

And no sooner they were off their shiff [2]

---

[1] Going on.   [2] Shift (miner's term), time underground.

Than the two of them there to climb the cliff
Under the Dragon's den, that was high
Up the mountain, and not very nigh
To the new workins—a lonely place,
And savage, if there ever was—
An ould shaft they'd worked out
Long ago, and nothin about,
No timb'rin nor the lck, just a hole,
And fifty fathom—no, not coal,
Lead, lead, like all these mines,
And worked accordin to the finds.
And when they're findin nothin more,
They never don't do nothin to her
To make her safe, no more till a quarry—
So that was the spot for Jack and Harry.

They were at it still when I come down
From the side of Snaefell, and I'll be bound
Me? yes, me ; from Sulby over,
Sulby Claddagh — Tommy Red-clover,
They were callin the chap, and married that day,
And axed to the weddin, and couldn stay,
And the sober amazin. So on and on,

Souljerin [1] lek, and thinkin the fun

I was leavin behind, till I come in my cruisin

Where the Northside gels is puttin their shoes on

When they're goin to Laxey fair—

Till they get up yandhar, aw bless ye ! as bare

As an egg : but there—aw I've seen them arrit [2]

Afore now, aw I have ! and some like a carrot

That red, and others like white stone

The smooth and the shiny—but—— lave it alone !

    Comin, I tell ye, and the sun was set,

And the moon was rose, but hidin yet

Aback o' Slieu Lhean, that was throwin a shaddhar

Terble black below me. The Laddhar

They're callin that slope. And I had to steer

Middlin careful, you know, to clear

The Dragon's den. So—no humbuggin !

I thought I heard a despard tuggin,

No thrashin, no smashin, no click o' the clogs,

No trampin like bulls, no raggin like dogs,

But *ugh-ugh-ugh*, like the chaps is goin

When they're working a blast-hole—it's lekly you're knowin—

<hr>

[1] Saumtering.   [2] At it.

Ugh-ugh-ugh· --- I didn lek it,

I tell ye, at all—how could you expeck it ?

How did I know that it wasn bogganes,

That's after takin ¹ up these glens,

Or the ould chap himself with some of his friends

Agate of their shindies—aw, might have been,

Might !   But I crep a bit nearer, and seen

There was two of them arrit ;² and the nearer I crep--

Harry ! Jack !

        Aw, at them I lep,

At them ! on them !   "Divils ! divils !

What's this? what's this? "   But they turned like swivels,

And the bank was givin way, and the muck

Rattlin down, the way it's shook

On a coffin at a funeral—

And the two of them twisted like a ball

Couldn get them out of grips,

Couldn—and Jack to stagger, and slips,

And Harry swings him out right over

The mouth of the pit, and could hardly recover

Hisself ; but held on—aw didn let go !

Wouldn ha' done it—no, no, no !

¹ Making their haunt.   ² At it.

Couldn, for the matter of that;

For Jack was stuck to him like a rat

To a terrier's nose. So I seen my chance,

And I gript this Harry—" Now then, once—

Twice—three times!" I said, and these rips

Come in on the grass, but still in grips.

And I couldn have done it, but Harry helped,

And glad enough. Aw, navar was whelped

A good-natureder chap! But done they were,

Done complate, aw, done I'll swear—

Not the half of a breath in the two of them.

So the moon come up, and I took a view of them—

" Well you're a pair of beauties!" I says;

"Come! drop these grips! I tell ye you'd best!"

But they couldn, no! they could only lie

In each other's arms.

    And Jack gave a sigh,

And so did Harry: but I got some water,

And I slished it on them. And Jack held tauter [1]

Till Harry; but at last they were sundhered,

And you'll aisy suppose it's me that wondhered

What divil's work they'd had in hand;

[1] Tighter.

And, as soon as ever they could stand,

I made the two of them look down

The shaft ; and they seen it lighted round

Very clear with the moon, that was shinin brave

And full by now　" If you're wantin a grave,

You'd batthar spake to the Clerk," I says,

" And get a comfortabler place

Than that," says I ; " it's like a well

Dug down to the deepest depths of hell."

And it really looked most horrible,

The black and the deep !　And Jack to shudder,

And turn away : and Harry's rudder

Not over studdy, but aised, it's lek,

Aised in his mind.

　　　　　　　　" And now be quick,

And on with your clothes ' "　For the chaps was bare

To the very buff　aw deed they were !

And the moonlight shinin on their skin—

These naked divils—astonishin !

" On with your boots and your clothes ! "　Aw, the one of
　　　them

Wouldn resist ! aw, I took the command of them

Fuss rate, I tell ye, uncommon though !

They were both that wake and 'zausted, ye know ;
And had to give in.

But Jack was mad,
And wouldn spake, like sulks he had—
Sullen, sulky.   But Harry, so soon
As he got his wind in a bit, was in tune
For a talk, and talked, and tould me the row,
And he said they'd been at it from seven till now ;
And what time would that be ?   And I looked at my
     watch—
The best of two hours !—" Why murder's a patch
To divils like you," I says.   " I doubt
It was swingin in and swingin out
All the time," says Harry, " wheelin
Like a windmill," says Harry, " toein-and-heelin,
Despard ! " he said.   *And him to be houlin
Jack right over, and rowlin and rowlin,
But wouldn dhrop him—no ! but try'n
To haul him back from the mouth of the mine.
But he'd stick his feet agin the bank,
And stiffen his body like a plank*
(" I see ye," I says), *and clitch and clutch,
And all along of a dirty wutch.*

"A dirty wutch ! what's that you say ? "

(Jack spoke at last).   " Round turn and belay ! "

Says I to Harry : " hould on at that !

That's somethin like business—I know the cat !

Now," I says, " let's hear it, my son ! "

Which immadient Harry done.

Says he—" She tould me that Nessy Brew

Was lovin me far more than you."

Jack danced, Jack danced—half joy, half rage,

Clasps Harry round the neck, I'll engage,

Like the hangman's hug, and cried and cried,

And kissed him, first on the one side,

And then on the other, as quick as a treadle

And Harry's big face as round as a griddle,

And the wondhrin there !   " I see it ! I see it ! "

Says Jack, " of coorse ! "   And a scream like a pewhit ;

And—— *the divil might give her a longish tether,*

But blow him ! he'd be even with her.

Well, I got them down to the washin floors

Very friendly ; and then these cures

Begun a schaemin what would they plan—

And—*Would they try the Ballawhane?*[1]

And axin me. "Aw, that's no use

At all," I says : "it's the very deuce,"

I says, "this wutchin—the horriderse[2] goin,

Black, yes, black." *But sure they were knowin*

The Ballawhane was workin the white?

"Aw, diffrin, bless ye! diffrin quite!

Lek cows and that—and gives you some sperrit,

Or harbs in a bottle ; and as soon as you'll gerrit[3]

In your fiss, the baste, that's very lekly

Miles away, is batthar toreckly.[4]

Aw I've seen the ould chap, and the big book

And the wise he'll talk, and the sollum he'll look—

Aw, diffrin, aw, that's understood—

Aw, doin good, doin good!

Aw, bless ye! the Ballawhane to wutch her!

Goodness grayshers! he couldn touch her!

Wutchin a wutch! aw, there's no sanse,

Sartinly not! Now, a little expanse,"

I says, "and you'll do her; yes, you will!

Do her as nice as pozzible—

---

[1] A celebrated herb doctor.   [2] Horridest.
[3] Get it.   [4] Directly.

Ned Kissack's gun—I know he'd lend her
Now then," I says, "what's goin to hender
But we'll make a silver bullet for her—
A silver bullet—there you've gorrer ' [1]
Melt some shillins- that's the way!
'Spansive? yes, but bound to pay!
That's your surt!   Now, let's go spy'n
The hedges on the Ballaquine,
And along to the Gill; and see if a hare
Or the Ick is often takin there—
The wutch—as sure as eggs is eggs,
Fire at her legs! fire at her legs!
And she'll disappear: but lo and behould!
Up to the Gill! and—*Makin so bould,*
How are ye, Mrs. Banks, this mornin !
Aw, limpin! aw, I give you warnin!
Limpin! of coorse—or a surt of a hop
Limpin, aye limpin all over the shop.
A silver bullet- eh?   Jack, my hearty!
That's the way to fix the party."

So we settled to try, and I down with my shillin,

---

[1] Got her.

Lek contributin—aw puffeck willin !

Contributin—lek these meetins they've got,

And *golly*[1] *this ! and golly that !*—

Missionaries—and round with the hat—

'Cited rather—and who would blame ?

And longin to be at the game.

" But," says Harry, " wutchin, I'll allow ;

But me or Jack ? "—" It's Nessy now,

Nessy," I says ; " aw that's the warp

She's agate of now ; so you'd batthar look sharp."

So we got the shillins, and we got the gun,

And we got a mould, and tuk and run

A bullet as big as a hymenanny,[2]

Fit to dhrop the divil's granny.

And started a hare the first thing ;

And Jack let dhrive, and she made a spring,

And away in the goss.   " Hit ! hit ! " says I,

" Hit in the thigh ! hit in the thigh ! "

And up to the Gill the way we planned ;

---

[1] Some faint echo of an anecdotic, nigger-dialectic " deputation."

[2] A large shell.

And there was Mrs. Banks as grand
As grand.   And—"What procures me the honour
Of this visit?"   A reg'lar Primer Donner—
Aw, it's her that could.   And "We want no talk,
Says Jack, "but just let's see you walk."

Aw, she up and made a run at us,
And we cut like the mischief; and she gave a cuss:
And then she laughed like fit to split
"She was never hit! she was never hit!"
Says Jack.   "No! no!" says I, "I'll swear
There's no mistake you hit the hare.
But that ould caillagh dhu!¹ what nex'!
Treminjis wutchin, xxx!"

And right I was; for there's wutches in
That actual don't care a pin
Not even for a silver bullet.
It's lek they've got an art to pull it
Aslant some way—aw black as tar!
Black! black! black! so there you are!

And was the coortin over and done!

¹ Black witch.

No, but, the winter comin on,

It had to be in the house, you see;

And the dooiney-molla for company

For ould Brew, that liked him well—

This Harry.   And sometimes they'd take a spell

At the paper they got, the *Sun*, or the *Times*,

Or Mona's *Harral*[1]—latthars, rhymes,

Speeches—not much odds to them

What they had.   And the ould chap's *hem!*

Ahem! dear me! and rubbin and rubbin

His specks; and the two of them goin a clubbin

Their heads together; but couldn make much of it—

Ould Brew, it's lek, could make some surt of Dutch of it;

But Harry could only scratch his nut—

Didn know B from a bull's foot.

And—"Can you see it, Harry?" and Harry pretendin,

And—*hadn azackly got his hand in,*

No—and another rub on his sleeve

At Brew, and eyein, and *what to believe?*

And—*was Harry humbuggin?* and 'spicious rather;

And then he'd dhrop it altogether.

But Harry could look, and Harry could smook,

[1] *Herald.*

Aw, bless ye! company for a duke
Was Harry—fuss-rate!   He'd a trick of spittin
He larned of me, thought nothin of hittin
A fly on the wall, or a spark in the chimbley,
Any distance you like, the nimbly
You never saw.   And the buzz and the bizz
And the 'twixt his teeth, and the fo'ce and the fizz
Like fireworks mostly : and his mouth like a flute,
All to make the puffeck skute [1]—
For a chap from Dalby that way—eh?
You'd hardly think now—what did ye say?
Learnt from me?   But a splendid scholar.
Aw, bless ye! baetin his masthar holler—
Yes, he did, aw beat complately—
Beat ; and amusin the old man greatly.
" Hit the rose on the side of that mug ! "
Or " Spit through the handle of yandhar jug
On the dresser there ! " or " Make a ring
Round yandhar cup ! "   He'd do the thing,
Would Harry, five times out of six.
But Nessy didn like such tricks ;
And she'd say   " Now what are ye after there?

----

[1] Squirt.

Behave, behave now, Henry Creer!"

And Harry to look a bit to one side,

And Brew to laugh till he fairly cried.

"What's the use o' talkin! chat![1]

Jack couldn do that! Jack couldn do that,"

The ould man would say, and "I hope he cudn,"

Nessy would say, "and I hope he wudn.

And even if so be it's allowed of,

It's nothin to be so very proud of;

No!" and *she wasn takin the huff!*

And *some people's manners was middlin rough.*

I believe in my heart the poor gel was ailin

All over some way, like a surt of a failin,

Yes, even her temper a little touched—

Wutched?—did ye say, of coorse she was wutched.

And wutched bad; why, a sweeter gel

Or a gennaler[2] never bruk the shell.

Nat'ral lovin, nat'ral wishin

To be kind, aw a beautiful dispogition.

But now she was often quick and cross,

Sharp and short lek—no, not sauce,

---

[1] Tut.   [2] More genial.

Not that! not that! but lek she'd been goin

Awakin up sudden, and hardly knowin

Where was she at all; and the white her face!

And when Jack was puttin his arm round her waist,

She'd start like needles runnin through her,

And away from him, and get to the door,

And look out, and come back, and her eyes to stare

Like seein somethin that wasn there

Despard uncomfible! aw, despard!

But special for Jack; for, if he whispered

In her ear—the way they will,

Lovers—or squeezed her hand a lill [1]

(And all in raison), she looked that scar'd

And that freckened, or else that stiff and that hard,

That Jack was nearly out of his mind.

And Brew would see, and pretend to be plyin

His spells—*just some of their little tiffs,*

Thinks Brew, and drops the paper, and sniffs;

And "Good-night!" he'd say, and "'Deed I've read

Till I'm tired urrov-massy," [2] and off to bed—

"They'll be makin it up all right," thinks Brew,

"When they're left to theirselves." But wouldn do.

---

[1] Little.   [2] Out of mercy – exceedingly.

For Harry would fall asleep, the baste,

And a big slop of a smile all over his face,

And snore like the roots of ragin thundher ;

And Nessy vexed, and 'deed no wondher,

That was used of the ould man's hollabaloo,

But didn like Harry's. And " I'll go too,"

She'd say ; and the loud this Harry roort [1]

It raelly wasn fit to coort—

You know the terble distressin it is.

So Jack to get some surt of a kiss,

Very skim-milky, very could !

And wakes up Harry, and off, poor sowl !

But the wuss of this wutch was Nessy was fond of her,

For of coorse she was gettin the upper hand of her

With the wutchin. But that wasn all, not a bit !

Fascernatin, is that it ?

Aw, you may call it any name,

Comedher, 'tractin,[2] all the same.

You see, she was used of her from a chile.

And, by gough, the woman had a style

That was off the common, knowin hapes

---

[1] Roared.   [2] Attracting.

I

Of sin, I doubt; and been in scrapes

And scrapes, it's lek.   But a surt of a flash with her,

And a cut, and a never-say-die, and a dash with her,

That was seemin grand to a country gel

Like Nessy, aye.   And the stories she'd tell,

Dear me ! and the 'sperience she had,

And the riddles and witty things that she said.

And Nessy, ye see, that innocent,

She didn twig the divilment---

Muck, man, muck, goin mixed with spice.

But divilment, no matter the nice,

Like some of these flowers you'll feed your eyes on,

Feed your belly?   look out for pizon.

    A bad stick ! a bad stick !

But terble bright ; and 'd give a slick

Of a polish lek to all her stuff,

And knew who she had, and 'd hould her luff,[1]

Manœuverin accordintly :

The woman was fuss-rate company

That's the words not mine ; no ! no !

Me? in a woman?   High or low,

[1] Knew how to steer.

Young or ould—I beg to state it—
The lek of yandhar I hate it, I hate it !

Fast she was—aw botheration !
She'd been in England in a sitchuation,
Lady's maid, or something o' the surt—
They're pickin up a dale of dirt
And mischief is them, aw I'll be bail !
And draggin it behind their tail,
When they're comin back to the Isle of Man—
Aw, bless ye ! I know them, I know them : bad scran
To the lek, says I.   They're callin it *life :*
But a gel that's to make an honest wife
For an honest man, for a chap that's worth,
He'd better give them a wide berth.

But of coorse she was seemin a terble swell
To Nessy, pretendin to feel with the gel,
Understandin all that was at her [1]
In her very sowl ; and chitter-chatter
About lovers and love.   Aw, Nessy thought
It was beautiful ! and the way she brought

[1] All that she had.

Everything to the one stress,

Like floodin her heart with happiness.

And the poethry ! aw dear, the nice !

And could sing—aw, bless ye ! a fine deep vice.

And whatever she said, or whatever she sung,

Had it at the tip of her tongue.

　Now Nessy was a gel that had got

A good head on her shouldhers, whether or not.

She was puttin very pretty talk urrov [1] her ;

But thinkin her aunt was nobbier far

Till her ; lek much more spicier :

Lek up-to-the-rigs.   And, you never can tell,

There's a bit of the divil in every gel—

Aw, there's no mistake they've gorrit, [2]

Yes, they have, and bless them for it !

　But that drunken ould brute ?　Now aisy ! aisy !

I know she wasn azackly a daisy

Of the field, this ould skunk ;

But still she wasn always drunk.

And these flighty people 'll have a go with them,

---

[1] Out of.　　　　　　　　　[2] Got it.

Bless my sowl! a kind of glow with them,

Like fine ould rum or somethin, is it?

Stirs you up, warms your gizzit [1]—

Potes is like that, and fiddlers is,

Play-acthors, singers, circusis—

They'll put a pinch of somethin tasty

In coortin and everything—don't be hasty!

Fond of liquor! I don't deny it—

Special when they haven to buy it—

Poor sowls!

   But how could Nessy be longin

For the woman that—— There you go ding-dongin!

Who talked of *longin?* *But the cruel she traited her*

About the ring, you'd think she'd ha' hated her.

Well lerrit [2] be wutchin, if you choose,

And nothin but wutchin—I don't refuse.

But maybe there's curiouser wrinkles

Till wutching even, my pennywinkles!

But drop it! drop it!

    Now Jack was a caution!

What d'ye think! he tuk a notion

He'd have the law of her! "Isn there laws

---

[1] Gizzard.   [2] Let it.

Agin wutches?" says Jack, "I'll trim her claws;

I'll go and see Kinley aburrit[1] at once."

He might as well have gone to France.

Says Kinley—"Do ye think I'm a d——d fool?"

Says Jack, "Well, no, sir, not of a rule—

But isn it law for a wutch to be rowlin

Down a brew[2] in a barrel, and bumpin and bowlin

Over the rocks, and nails that teases

And rags and cuts her all to pieces—

Pintin innards? Lek they done at Slieu Whallion

Afore now. Well, we've got an ould rapscallion

At Laxdale. . . ." But Kinley got despard impatien'—

"Well then, would it be suffayshin[4]

To burn her?" says Jack. " Be off, you brute!"

Says Kinley, "you donkey! you thundh'rin toot!"

"Is that your 'pinion? and what are ye chargin?"

Says Jack. My gough! you may aisy imargin

Ould Kinley! and turns to the clerks, and he roors—

" Pack this bumpkin out of doors!"

And bundled out like a sack o' potatis -

Says Jack— " I've got[5] a 'pinion gratis."

[1] About it.   [2] Hill.

[3] A mountain near Peel, in the Isle of Man; the legend referred to is well known.   [4] Sufficient.   [5] Got.

So it was woe Bethsaida! woe Chorazin!

"Jack," says I, "will you go to the Pazon?

You've had a shot at mostly everything posbil,

You've tried the law, let's try the gospel.

Let's go to church to-morrow," I said,

" And hear the Pazon goin ahead.

And after he's done the sarvice we'll foller him

Into the house, and then we'll collar him."

So the three of us went—that's Jack and me,

And Harry! yes, Harry, unfortnitly—

I wasn much used of church, I'll confess,

Not them times—aw, younger, yes—

In the Quire, and the Pazon theer—

Good Lord! how I loved him! aw dear, aw dear!

But knockin about, and often at say,

Aw, a lill church 'll go a long way.

But still I was useder till Harry, that never

Went to any place whatever—

A reg'lar haythen surt of a chap,

Lek these Dalby fellows is very ap',[1]

Ap' enough—and hadn no notion

---

[1] Apt (to be).

How to behave, and a surt of a ocean
Of spit at this divil ; the whole of the pew
Nearly swimmin—aw it's true ! it's true !
And 'd mark some speck in the grain, or a knot
In the timber, and fire a splandid shot.
I know he could do it—of coorse he could—
Bless ye ! that was understood.
And I warned him once, and I warned him twice—
I did, I did ! and it isn nice.
No it isn, in church, eh ? what ?
It's a dirty, savage thing is that.
The Clerk's wife had to clane it out
Agin the next Sunday—treminjus stout
That woman was—and then the churchwardens—
Kneale Ballagill, and Stole the Gardens
Made a presantment—is that it ?
That they couldn pozzibly do with spit
In the church like yandhar ; but just to annoy
The Pazon, because he was takin joy
Of the leks of me   I knew them, blow them !
And so did everybody know them.

But however we got him middlin quite[1]

[1] Quiet.

Sittin there. I took a delight

To hear the Pazon readin the sarvice ;

Lek, you know, a lill bit narvous—

Aw, beautiful ! For praechin—— well——

I was likin him terrible ;

But others was sayin he hadn the power :

And of coorse he cudn go on by the hour

Like these Locals and that, nor he cudn shout

And rag, and fling his arms about

Like a windmill theer, and his body goin drivin

Half urrov[1] the pulpit—and how they're contrivin

To keep their balance God only knows,

And sweatin and stranglin in their clothes

Most awful they are ; and " Awake ! awake !

Ye sinners ! " and roors. But delicake—

That was the Pazon—not raw, but ripe,

And mallow, like berries, like a aisy pipe,

That draws like a baby the smooth it's goin—

There's some that's bad to rattle and groan

Boosely—what ? just wantin clanin—

Aye ! But the Pazon that putty[2] strainin

Like God was takin him for a flute,

---

[1] Out of.   [2] Pretty.

And playin on him—*tootle-toot?*
Not Him! but lovely music, clear
And sweet.   You'd think, if you could hear
An angel smilin, it 'd be rather
Like that—— what?   " I'll go to my father,"
It's sayin theer, "and sinned," d'ye see!
" Against Heaven," aye! "and before thee,
And no more worthy to be callin
Thy son."   And " Dearly beloved," and fallin
Down on their knees.   And "no health in us,"
And "lost sheep," and wuss and wuss.
And then the Pazon on his own hook,
And the sollum, and the lovely look
On his dear ould face—and the surt of a tenor,
And "desireth not the death of a sinner"—
Like just a mossel higher—aye!
Aw fit to make a body cry—
Fit enough ; and safter[1] and safter,
And "that the rest of our life hereafter——
My gough! like drops upon a wound,
And all "through Jesus," you'll be bound.

[1] Softer.

The way he had! the way he had!

Say the words now, James, good lad!

Say them! try!—you can't? no, no!

Nor you, nor the one of us.   We must turn to

And be like the Pazon, that's it, Jem—

Innocent and pure like him.

But O the hard! O night and day!

"O Lamb of God, that takest away

The sins of the world, have mercy upon us!"

(Kneel, men, kneel!) "have mercy upon us!"

    "O Christ, hear us!

    O Christ, hear us!

    Lord, have mercy upon us!

    Lord, have mercy upon us!

    Christ, have mercy upon us!

    Christ, have mercy upon us!

    Lord, have mercy upon us!

    Lord, have mercy upon us!"

    (Silence for a time.)

I'll go on.   The service was over for sure,

And then we in on the back door,

And axed would the Pazon see us two,

Not Harry of coorse, that cudn do
With the like o' yandhar, hadn the wit in—
Bless ye ! a good-sized field to spit in
Was Harry's notion, and, rocks or reels,
The Pazon's fields was beautiful fields.

But the Pazon was in his study theer,
Sittin in the arm-cheer,
And the servant brought the two of us in,
And sniffed, and cut, but lizzenin
Outside no doubt, aw, lizzened,
Aw, as sure as she was chrizzened—
Bless ye ! how could she help it—eh ?
Just natheral, as you may say—
Natheral.   So—" Pazon," I says,
" Here's Jack Pentreath, that'll not take rest
About wutches," I says ; and I up and tould
All the jeel ;[1] and the Pazon to fould
His hands in a book, and as aisy as aisy,
And no hurry whatever ; and Jack half crazy,
And " Go on then, Tom ! go on ! go on ! "
And cudn wait till I was done ;

[1] Damage, trouble.

Like a thunderstorm! aw fire and hail!

And "Yes, Pazon Gale!" and "No, Pazon Gale!"

And lovin Nessy, and Nessy him,

And as happy as Jerusalem,

Till this dirt begun her divil's tricks,

And wutchin the gel, "and puttin betwix

Hal Creer and me," he says, "thal was allis

The best of friends;" *and the gallis, the gallis*

Was too good for the lek, and if they got

Their rights, it's lek they'd find it hot—

"Hot," he says, "rather hot, rather hot,"

Says Jack; *but however, and whether or not,*

They'd get it at last aback of the bars

Of hell, these divil's sassingers,

Fryin, yes! But could nothin be done

Afore that to stop their carryin on?

And—"Look here, Pazon, here's a go!

Think of Nessy—as pure as the snow,

And as sweet that shuggar cudn be sweeter,

And this ould scoundhrel, this ould blue Peter

Of a rag of a vagabone to pizon

The loveliest craythur ye ever set eyes on!

Pizon! pizon! sartinly!

Body and sowl—machree![1] machree!

Pazon, Pazon! it shudn be!

It shudn! it shudn!"—"What pizon then?"

Says the Pazon, " what pizon is it that's in,

Jack?" he says.   "You surely don't think

She's givin Nessy stuff to drink,

Harbs or the lek?"—"No, no!" says Jack;

"My gough! she's on another tack

Altogether.   What odds' the drinkin?[2]

Pizonin, pizonin like winkin;

Sartinly!" *not givin, but doin,*

That was it—at the full moon—

Harbs—and what was to hindher her? d—— it!

(The Pazon looked funny.)   *Did he think they'd ram it*

Down a gel's throat?   My gough! what sense!

" Harbs! charms! did ye ever?—go to France!"

"Now Jack," I says, "you'll spake respactful

To the Pazon," I says.   "Harbs! many a sackful

I've seen at her," says Jack; "but dose

And drug the gel!—But the Pazon knows

Of coorse—no frankincense nor myrrh

Wasn that; and ask your pardon, sir—

---

[1] My heart.   [2] What difference does the drinking make?

Brewin, that's it! and these divil's birds,

And the evil eye, and sayin the words,

And the strength, and the steam, and the black art—

And lawyers—bless ye! takin their part—

Lawyers—much on the same hand.

But the Pazon's the man! the Pazon's the man!

Eh, Tom? Let the Pazon go to work!

That's the boy that'll draw their cork!"[1]

"Respactful," I says, "then, Jack, if ye plaise;

Respactful, respactful!" And the Pazon to raise

His eyes a bit; and—"Do you believe

In this nonsense?" he says; and lek to reeve

A surt of a laugh through his shouldhers lek.

And—"Thomas," he says, "aw well I'd expeck

Better of you."—"What for then, Pazon?"

Says I, "if you'll excuse me as'in."

But Jack gave no time—"A Bible!" he says,

"A Bible! a Bible! chapter and vess!

Here you are! do you want to make fun of me?"

And the leaves goin flyin, and "Deuteronomy,"

And—*A wutch shall be put to death*—very well;

[1] Triumph over them.

And whips him over to Samuel—

"Wutches!" he says, "all right! all right!

And risin the ould man in the dead of the night,

Ordered at [1] Saul, ordered at Saul—

Sartinly, and hadn no call,

Not the laste."—"The witch of Endor,"

Says the Pazon; and "Yes! and how he'd befriend her,

And *no punishment*, he says; and look!

Look here!" says Jack, and shoves the book

Under the Pazon's very nose,

"Look here, man! look! and Samuel's ghose

Ascendin urrov the earth—see, see!

Like gods." "You're makin very free,

Jack," I says; "respactful now!

Respactful, will ye!"—"Stop your row!

Says Jack. "*Lek gods*, it's sayin—what?

Eh, Pazon? But Samuel gev it him hot,

Didn he, Pazon? Hev ye forgot?

Lizzen, lizzen! vess [2] twenty-two :

And she made him ate his supper too—

To be sure!

Twenty-three, twenty-four

[1] By.   [2] Verse.

And she hasted and killed a fat calf—

See, see! and *unleavened bread thereof—*

There ye are! *went away that night—*

Fuss [1] of Samuel, twenty-eight.

Now then! now then! *No wutches, eh?*

No wutches, Pazon? Is that what you say?

In the Bible?" And *goodness grayshers!*

What was the gud o' Pazons and praechers,

If they were goin a denyin the very texes

In the Bible itself?" And—"The laste ye expecks is

Give in to the Bible!" And the Pazon smilin

Very paceful. "Well, don't be vi'len'!" [2]

Says the Pazon, "but let me 'splain the thing."

Aw Jack to sulk, and Jack to fling—

And *what was these Pazons but all a sham?*

And didn care a twopenny d—n!

"Be quite!" I says, "be quite now, Jack!

Look here! we'll have no disrespack

To Pazon Gale! No cussin here!

No cussin before the Pazon, theer!"

'Deed I spoke savage; for, traycle or botter, [3]

---

[1] First.   [2] Violent.   [3] Treacle or butter.

Manners is manners—that's my motter.

But bless ye ! the Pazon didn take

The smallest notice ; he'd hev gev[1] him a shake

Sure enough, if it hedn ha' been

The terble bothered and 'cited he seen

Poor Jack was—for ye musn suppose

The Pazon 'd hide his head under the clothes

When cussin was goin—not him !   What ! cussin

Before the Pazon ?   My gough ! ye dussin—

The chaps wudn have it !   It wasn him,

But us, by G—d.   It's limb from limb

We'd ha' tore the divil that dar'd to 'sult

Ould Pazon Gale.   But Jack was pull't[2]

Very sore in his heart ; and the Pazon was kind,

And so, ye see, he didn mind—

No—

        And then he 'splaint[3] and 'splaint,

Aw, uncommon !   And   *The Testament*,

And the Ould and the New, and close akin,

But still for all the differin—

And dispensin and that.   And all about ghoses,

And divils, and Samuel, and Moses ;

---

[1] Have given.   [2] Pulled.   [3] Explained.

And *the power of the evil one,* and them dirts

That was *possessin* people, unclean spir'ts,

And *spir'ts of infirmity*—just so ;

And that muck of divils that was *suffered to go*

Into the pigs, that was feedin away—

Muck [1] to muck ! lek a body might say—

And *drowned in the waters.*   And Christ to send them

About their biznuss, and take and pin them

In the only place they gor a right to,

And sure enough that's hell.   And they'll try to

Ger [2] out for a sthrowl, no doubt ; but they can't—

And their power is gone ; and no matter the haunt

Or the used of [3] a place, or a pesson's body,

They're done complate.   Some niddy-noddy

Of a poor craythur you'll be seein still

On the counthry goin ; but unpozzible

For these divils to touch them, bein innocent—

Wutches ! no !   But others rent

With fire and fury, and they're callin,

Insane, and that, and shoutin and bawlin—

Aw, as mad as brute bases—

---

[1] Pig (Manx).   [2] Get out.

[3] How much they are used to.

But just a disase like other disases.

But *woutches!* we've got nothin to say with—

Wutches! They're tuk and done away with

Altogether ; got the sack ;

And Christ that done it, and that's a fact !

And *Baalim and Ashtaroth,*

Heaven's queen and mother both—

Somethin like that—but I'll take my oath

A Roman? the Pazon ! God bless your sowl :

Not him ; but, if I may make so boul',

Just houl' your jaw !   And—*The Libye Ammon,*

The chap with the horns ; and ould *Mammon,*

That must ha' been a surt of a fool,

With his eyes on the floor for the fond of the gool—

Hapes—but druv away like chaff

Afore the babe that was born in the laf'[1]

At laste, the manger—and no use a' rebellin—

That's the way the Pazon was tellin.

The Bible? No ; but a blind ould party

By the name o' Milton—blind, but hearty ;

Gor[2] an eye inside of him theer,

---

[1] Loft.   [2] Got.

Somewhere or another, an eye that clear
It could split the bottom of darkness in two,
And hev[1] a view, aw, he'd hev a view,
Fuss-rate, would Milton; aw, he wudn fail!
But the Bible—— But the Pazon was thinkin a dale
Of this Milton, and the grand he wrote—
A pote, ye know, of coorse, a pote.
But still, for all—— a pote, yis, yis!
But somethin about it in Genesis.

Beautiful the Pazon purrit.[2]
But, bless ye! I might take and worret
My brains till next week, and I cudn give it
The way the Pazon did—like a rivet,
The close and the sthrong—uncommon though!
And still, for all, was there wutches or no—
Aw, my gough! it's hard to be sayin—
Aye—but seemin terble plain
When the Pazon was agate of the arguin talk;
Nor me, nor even Jack didn balk
The Pazon, nor never stirred nor winced,
But let him go on; but whether convinced—

---

[1] Have.   [2] Put it.

It isn me—my goodness, no!
But terble quite and pleasant though.

And then the Pazon said he'd spake
To Nessy herself; and *he hoped she'd take*
Heart, he said; "for, Jack," he says,
"If you're lovin each other in truthfulness ;
If your love is rael, if your love's *sincere*
(He was fond of the word), then never fear!
There's no power on earth, or anywhere else,
That'll harm ye, no!"   And the ould eyes fills—
Aw, they did! aw they did, and the hands was
    gript,
And Jack in the slush of tears, and slipt
On his knees—poor sowl! aw, feelin! feelin!
And the Pazon blessed him where he was kneelin—
Sobbed, did Jack ; and "You'll spake to her, yis!
You'll spake, you'll spake!" and sobbed, and ris.[1]
And out on the door, and off with us there,
And the two of us cryin like fools we were—
"D——d fools," says Harry, when he met us—
But Harry was Harry, so that didn fret us—

    [1] Rose.

"D——d fools, is it? well grantit! grantit!

But lave us, Harry." So Harry slantit.

And the Pazon kep his word, for he went

The very next day to see Nessy, and spent

The best of an hour with her there, and he tould her

All about wutches; and a mind to scould her

For the fearful she was: but all he done

Was spoke to her, and made the run [1]

Much the same he did with us—

And Nessy cryin fit to bus'—

And about the *power; they cudn hev it,*

These wutches, no! And who was to gev it?—

Most of them wake in their intelleck;

But others wicked; and the faymale seck

In general, the Pazon said—

Aye, *wrong in the head, wrong in the head.*

But mischievous enough was a wutch—

Sartinly—and spacial for such

That believed in the lck. But believe them not,

And where's their power? it's gone like a shot.

"It's you that gives them the power," he says,

---

[1] Took the same line.

" By believin in all this wickedness —

Power? It's you that's 'sponsible for it ;

Don't give them the power, and they hevn gorrit.[1]

Poor thing !" he says, "poor thing ! poor thing !

Poor Nessy then !" And the hands to wring

At[2] Nessy—aye—" And your aunt," he said :

" Your aunt ! aw dear ! it's very bad —

Very bad, and very hard "

But the door of messy wasn barred

Agin the lek. And then he tuk

A little prayer, and Nessy shuk

All over ; but got more pacefuller.

And then she said—" Will you spake to her,

Masthar Gale?" she says. Aw, his lip was goin,

But never a word, and never no knowin

Azackly what was arrim[3] his head

All stooped, you know. But at last he said –

" I will"—very low, like a surt of a pride,

That humble and that dignified.

And the hat and the stick ; and Nessy freckened

To see him like yandhar. Now it's general reckoned

----

[1] Got it.　　　　[2] On the part of.

[3] At him (what was the matter with him).

That Pazons is special—what, special? my gough!

A Pazon can spit, and a Pazon can cough.

What is it botherin you and me

In our sowls? We know we've done wrong, d'ye see!

Give it a word now! chrizzen [1] it, chrizzen it!

In our sowls, in our sowls, man—Conscience, isn it?

Conscience—sartinly. And the same

With Pazons. *Pazons feelin shame?*

To be sure! aw, good enough some of them;

But still a conscience! You're thinkin it's rum of them?

They should be angels altogether?

But bless ye! bless ye! just considher——

Or—— drop it! Anyway, I'll be bail

There was conscience plenty in Pazon Gale.

And he knew he shud ha' spoke to this beauty

Long afore, lek bein his duty

As clear as clear: but didn, no!

That's the way—just so! just so!

The delicake—that's the way he spar'd her:

Bless ye! the delicaker the harder!

Isn it? reg'lar? the harder to spake

To such dirts, the harder to have or to make

---

[1] Christen.

With their doins, the natheral to keep

Urrov[1] their road, lek the way with a sweep,

And his rope, and his brush, and his bag of shoot.

But wrong, I tell ye, and the Pazon knew't.

So that's the way his countenance fell

Lek you'll obsarve before this gel—

Remindin me of Peter though,

And Jesus to look, and the cock to crow ;

But cussed did Peter, but went out in the rain.

And wept bitterly, it's sayin.

Yes, I've seen some of your touch-me-nots

Of Pazons, machine-made Pazons—lots !

Castins o' Pazons, that moulded and squared,

Blackleaded and polished, that how are they rared

I don't know in my senses, no more till I'd know

How a stove'd be rarin—toe to toe !

Aw beautiful ! but rared they ar'n,

But that prim and that puffeck the divil dar'n

Come nigh them, it's lek.   And they never done wrong,

And they never done right . . . ding-dong, ding-dong !

Ah, my men ! when I'll die, when I'll die !

[1] Out of.

Who'll meet me yandhar up in the sky?
Who'll hould me theer that I can stand?
Who'll take my hand? who'll take my hand
Afore all'that glory? Not one of them—
No, no! but him! but him! but him!

The dear ould head . . . he stooped it, did he?
Well, but off to see the widdy—
This Banks—that very minute, aye!
But never saw her . . . why then, why?
Never saw her, that's it!
Never, never! but wait a bit!

She wasn at home when the Pazon knocked,
No answer, at laste; and the door was locked,
And Job away at the Clague's; and so
Of coorse the Pazon had to go.
But tried again next day; but never
No Mrs. Banks, that dodged him clever,
You'd be thinkin—what? aw, well, well, well!
And next day, and next day; and it's hard to tell—
Weeks, it's lek—the Pazon was off
Every day to yandhar crof';

Weeks and weeks—and no use ;

And poor Job tuk in at Brew's ;

And wond'rin greatly what had become

Of the mother ; but still he had a home,

Of coorse ; but terrible forsaken

Was Job, and sorrowful, and takin

Up on the mountains and callin, callin

"Mother ! mother !"   And chaps that was trawlin

Down on the shore would feel a let,[1]

And think they'd got her in the net—

But no !   And Brew though, very kind :

And—"Never mind ! never mind !

She'll be in Ramsey."   And axin theer,

And Douglas, you know, and everywheer,

Till at last says Brew, " I'll wager she's gone

To Liverpool ;" and " Lave her alone,

And she's all right."

And Jack to coax

This Nessy to marry him ; and little jokes

And a bit cheerfuller ; but wudn consent :

And - "Oh, I can't ! O Jack, I can't !"

And *the cruel it was of him to persist,*

---

[1] Hindrance (something that caught the net).

And shiver, and hide her head in his breast.

And never no forrader, and *Harry*,

The dooiney-molla?   Of coorse, to marry,

And to marry at once—" What capers ! blow it ! "

Marry away! how the deuce would she know it?

"Chance it ! " says Harry, "chance it ! "—" Take care,"

Says Nessy, "what you're talkin there !

This strong wutchin is hard to clane

Urrov[1] things ; it gets in the grain,

The very subjecs,[2] lek no bleachin 'll fly[3] it,

Nor nothin else won't purify it.

It's all about in the fields and the bushes,

You'd think you could see it among the rushes,

Creepin, crawlin, like a blue mist,

Like the breath of some spir't."   And she took and kissed

Poor Jack, that looked lek rather onaisy,

I tell ye.   But Harry jumped like crazy—

" You're right," he says, " I'm feelin it . . . what ?

All round me," he says ; " it's could and it's hot,

And it's stickin all over, like these webs," he says,

" That's spun in the air ! I'll cut urrov this,"

Says Harry—I'll cut . . . I will though ! " and off,

---

[1] Out of.   [2] Substance.   [3] Make it fly.

That Nessy cudn help but laugh—
Poor sowl!

But when the summer come round,
And the apples in blossom, and all the ground
Speckled with daisies, then Harry tried
To get them to do the coortin outside,
The way they were used.   For the chap had a notion
That the lovely smell, and the draught, and the motion
Of the wind through the trees, and the sweet and the fresh,
And the wholesome lek would unfasten the mesh
Of this divil's net that their hearts was caught in.
But Nessy wudn ; she said—*they oughtn,
Nor no pleasure nor nothin,* she said,
Till they'd know at laste was she live or dead—
This Banks.   *Believin in witches still?*
Of coorse! of coorse! dear me! they will—
The women—and *me?*   Yes me, and you,
For the matter of that.   So don't give *sthoo*[1]
Quite so hasty.   *The Pazon* you're sayin?
Fuss-rate! fuss-rate!   But you know what I mane—
The Pazon was arguin capital—
Arguin—but that's not all,

---

[1] Chase, find fault.

Isn arguin—it grips

The head of a fellow ; but what is it rips

Your very sowl ? What is it gives way

Inside ye, sinks ye, scuttles ye,

Falls urrov ye like a false bottom ?

That's the thing ! ye fancy ye got him,

Because he don't answer ye ! answer your granny !

Isn it natur that's in ? how can he

Go agin her ? Take pitchforks to her,

You'll never put her to the door—

Never ! natur ! bred in the blood !

Well, it's not natheral ye cud.

Two years went on, and not a word

About this Mrs. Banks was heard

At the Ballaquine, nor anywhere else,

Not a word : and boys and gels

Was pairin off, and weddins goin ;

But Jack and Nessy wasn showin

No signs at all. But lizzen, my men !

I tould ye about the Dragon's Den,

That was high up on the mountain side ;

And the ould shaft, that was op'nin wide

At the foot of the slock [1]—and gave up workin

I don't know the years.   Well now then herkin !

The Directors tuk a notion they'd try

This shaft again : and Captain Spry

Agate o' the search ; and tuk a gang,

And Jack was one, and I'll be hang

If they didn take Job to help to carry

Their tools, or the lek o' yandhar.   And Harry—

Harry was there.   And Job was lettin

Down with a rope, for the way he'd be gettin

Some candles lit on the first level,

For to light them, ye know.   And a bank of gravel,

And then the shaft went farther down.

So Job was gropin, and got his ground,

And lit a candle.   And they heard a cry

Most terrible they did.   And Spry

Gave orders at once for Jack to be low'rt

Down to the level, and just to report

What was the matter.   And so he done·

And what aw, what did he find but the son

And the mother ?   And Job had fainted dead—

Poor thing ! and there he was laid

By the side of the bones and the skull.   For ye see

[1] Hollow.

He knew her by the clothes—machree! [1]

Machree! machree! And in her hand

She was claspin an 'arb—I don't understand

Azackly what; but I'm tould it's knowin

For the used at [2] these wutches, and hardly growin

Anywhere but round this shaft.

And that's the way, lek follerin her craft,

She must have gone prowlin up yandhar place,

And missed her footin—and God's grace

Is for all, for all! But the 'arb had struck

A root in the gravel, and her hand was stuck

To the soil; and they had to tear it out—

Just fancy what a place to sprout!

But these dirts . . . but lave it. And Jack, though, Jack—

He sent Job up first: and then a sack

Was low'rt to him; and every pin of her,

And clout, and whatever there was in [3] of her,

It was Jack, I tell ye, that gathered them all,

And made the signal for the men to haul;

And come up last himself, as game,

And divil a word; but his face all aflame

With the joy, you'd think. For he knew what 'd happen

---

[1] My heart.   [2] As being used by.   [3] *In* is superfluous

Soon enough now. But when the ould cap'n
Said, "Jack, my lad, that's a good job for you—
You'd better go tell it to Nessy Brew "—
Aw, bless ye! that was too much for him—what?
It floored him just the same he'd been shot,
And he fell like a corp. Then the men stood round,
And never a sound, never a sound!
Till Jack come to in the teems of tears
And sobs. And bless my sowl then! wheer's
The man cud ha' stood it? I know I cudn—
Joy?—it was joy: but tuk that sudden
And—— well, well, well—they formed in a line,
And they carried her to the Ballaquine
In puffeck silence—the wutch was dead;
They knew what they had, they knew what they had.

Next day the bell was toullin for her;
And maybe it oughtn; but sorrer is sorrer
After all; and God is a God
Of mercy— yes! I broke a sod
Of her grave myself; and the woman was buried—
The lightest coffin ever I carried.
And the Pazon read the sarvice—yis!

And—" Our dear sister," what's this it is?

Aye, . . . and the . . . " sure and sartin hope "—

Well, I won't say nothin—God gives the scope,

Not man; it's Him that slacks to us,

And rides us aisy—and well He does.

    Anyway we buried the woman,

And the wutchin with her. So now what's comin?

Comin? What? Why Jack of coorse,

And Nessy—aw, as sure as sure's.

Happy, I tell ye, sartinly!

And me to church with them, it's aisy to see.

And nice she looked, and nice she was—

And summer for winter, and heat for frost;

And the dooiney-molla all in his glory;

And the club bruck up, and the end of the story—

Jack Pentreath—you'll remember him—

And Nessy Brew—Just douse that glim!

THE INDIAMAN

AYE! exactly—that's the name—

Fanny Graeme, Fanny Graeme—

Come aboord in the Prince's dock—

Loadin theer—and caught her frock

In the gangway—the crooky it was put—

And a slip and a skip, and a twist of her foot,

And fell in his arms—*Whose arms?* you shoutit?

That shows you don't know much about it —

Who and what, and where and when—

Avast these quashtins![1] Peter's then—

Peter's arms—that's Peter Young,

Peter the printice, Peter the Tongue

That's what we called him, bein despard slippy,

And quick as light, and droppy and drippy

With the honey feathered on its pint,

[1] Questions.

And the curl, and the click, and the swingin jint—

Thriddle-thraddle; beef or pork,

You couldn touch him with the talk.

Had to hommer him—that was all,

Hommer him—and then to fall

Right in his arms, lek aboord a wreck,

And his arms round her waist, and her arms round his
neck,

Houldin on most terblc though :

And me to take her very slow,

As dignified as dignified,

And studdy her agin [1] the side—

And—*Was she hurt?* and as red as a buckie,[2]

And tould that chap to cut his lucky—

Unknownst, of coorse—just whisp'rin theer,

Like redhot sarpints in his ear.

So the divil cut, but gave a look,

Aw my gough! like print in a book—

This Peter—like print, havin tongues in his eyes,

And everywhcer, lerr [3] alone the size,

---

[1] Steady her against. .   [2] IIip, berry of the dog-rose.   [3] Let.

And the light that was at them [1]—aw, by jingers !
These deaf-and-dumb chaps, with their fingers—
Aw bless ye ! they might ha' gone to school to him—
Tallagraphs was only a fool to him.
Now what could you do with this divil's kin ?
Hommerin, just hommerin.

So I took the lady to her cabin,
And he turned, and another look like stabbin,
For me, you know ; so took and went,
And gave it him immadient—
Aw, wanted it bad !   And—*who was he*
To be buckin up to the quality—
A pup like him—and this and that—
Oh ! he was on me like a cat—
And—*Who was he !* and *he'd have me to know*—
And   *a gentleman's son*—"Woho ! woho !"
I says, " My lad ; is it tongue that's in ? "
And when I begun I did begin—
Hommerin ! yes, hommerin.

But the deed was done, whichever way,

_____
[1] Which they had.

Couldn ha' been done-er—— eh?

Comedher?[1] bless ye! him or her—

Couldn ha' been comedherer!

A chance, a glance, a touch, a breath,

And there you're lovin unto death—

Strange! and others—I'll defy them!

Do what you like with them, splice them, tie them—

Every knot, and Pazon and Clerk,

And all the boults in Noah's ark—

Bless your sowl! just differin total—

Lek it's often with things that's poured in a bottle—

Shake them, shake them the vicious you can!

You'll navar mix them—will ye, Dan?

Just so with pessins—for all your bother,

They'll navar be nothin to one another.

That's the way; and listen to me—

Before the pilot left—d'ye see?

That soon, bedad! they'd got to talkin—

The cheek of the chap! and her too—shockin!

Shockin—— And still it wasn bould,

Nor imprint, no, upon my sowl!

[1] Charm, spell.

An innocenter thing you navar,

But lively.   And so, goin down the river,

The pilot seen ; and, just he was steppin

Over the rail, he turns to the Cap'n,

And a cough, and a wink like squoze through a eyelet—

"Mind your printice !" says the pilot.

"Mind your printice !"   Aw, I got a view of them,

If the Captain didn ; and, behould ye ! the two of them,

Him in the mizen shrouds, and her

In the starboard quarter-gallery there—

And her lookin sorrowful, and him lookin sorrowful,

And her lookin plaised, and him lookin plaised,

Till I tell ye then I was nearly crazed ;

And hailed him, and down with him quick enough,

And run him forrard by the scruff—

Aw the sorrowful ! the forsoken !

Just lek you'd think their hearts was broken—

And then the smilin that 'd be goin—

Aw dear ! the ways—you're navar knowin—

Botherin one another—what ?

Aw botherin, taezin, all to·that—— [1]

[1] Etc.

And still no harm—aw, I wouldn say't,

Nor I wouldn think it—wait then, wait!

Imps of things! But raison is raison,

And cautious of coorse is allis in saison.

Cautious—that was the Skipper's word,

And had me in his cabin, and heard

All I had to say ; and says he,

" Mr. Baynes," he says, " you'll see

To this," he says, " Mr. Baynes," he says,

" And you'll be cautious, cautious—yes,

Very cautious," he says ; " take pains,"

He says, " and be cautious, Mr. Baynes—

I'm trustin altogether to you,

Quarter-master," he says ; " the crew

Is excellent," he says—— " ahem——

But of coorse my officers is them

I'm bound to trust, and allis will."

Aw, bless your sowl! the 'spectable,

Them times—*what me !* yes, me, bedad !

And rather a fatherly way I had,

Fatherly—just so, just so—

Fatherly uncommon though,

The fatherly you wouldn think ;
And tuk a notion, and gave up the drink—
My goodness ! the clear my head was then—
Head and heart and all, my men—
Clear as a bell—as a bell though, yis—
Bless my sowl ! the nice it is !

Clear—that's it, lek clear in the head—
And—— fatherly, fatherly, was it I said ?
Fatherly—I'll tell ye what,
I belave there's hapes of chaps like that—
Navar had a chick or a chile,
Nor the name of it ; and all the while
They've got the father in them that strong
That they crave and crave, and they long and they long,
And they're tuk with it that terrible
That they'll have it some way—aye, they will—
And anything young that's comin near them
They're just for worshippin—navar fear them !
Who makes it work in them like leaven ?
Isn't it God, our Father in heaven ?
Oh yes it is—it's Him, I expeck—
I was allis terble fond of the lek.

But still, a father, I don't care who,

Should have the 'torrity [1] with him too,

The 'torrity, for all the kind,

And the touch-me-not, and the draw-the-line,

And "aisy-all!" and give them slaps,

And hould them in, and his heart perhaps

Just meltin in his body like dips

For the way he's feelin for these rips—

But still, of coorse, as firm and stately—

Aw, that's where I was bet complately—

Bet, I tell ye, yes, yes, yes—

I was too soft. "Be cautious!" he says ;

And cautious I was ; but I couldn be rocks,

And I couldn be ropes, and I couldn be locks,

And keys, and patent-safeties—what ?

And boults, and bars—And her to get

The fond of me, whatavar made her—

Aw the little desperader !

Well, ye know, this is the way it began—

Did ye ever see an Indiaman ?

One of the reggilar ould model,

---

[1] Authority.

Diddle-daddle, all a-straddle,
Like a turkey-cock.   They're much more simple
Is big ships now: but Solomon's temple,
With carvin and gildin, and goodness knows!
Knobs and bobs, and Jachin and Boze,
Wasn nothin to yandhar craft;
With a Tower-o'-Babel risin aft,
And windhers like a 'sarvatory,
And galleries there, just story on story,
Like summer-houses goin a-cockin—
Aw, most horrible! most shockin!
No room to work, and still a waist
Like a haggard, or a market-place,
Or a church—and doors and doors, treminjis!
And allis comin off the hinges.

So there ye are! and gettin together,
And hidin, bless ye! just consedher—
And so many places where they *cud* be—
How could I guess the place they *wud* be?
And when I'd catch them, there'd be the one
Lookin out at the horizon
As straight and as studdy as a beadle,

And the other workin away with her needle—
Very silent—

       Fanny Graeme—

Aw that's the name though, that's the name—
A Colonel's daughter, the Captain stated,
And sent to England to be eddicated,
And just left school, and her uncle put her
Aboord with us, bein bound for Calcutta,
And the father "a terble swell out there,"
Says the Captain, "it's very particular,"
And—*for me to mind my p's and q's well,*
And—*much more cautiouser till usual—*

      That was the Captain : and so I did.
But then these things and the way they were hid.
One evenin I caught them under the lee
Of the long-boat there—the 'dacity !
Quiet enough, and very proper
In regard of their conduck and that ; but a stopper
Had to be put; so I signed him to me,
And made him go forrard straight, and, blow me !
If I didn tan him that time well—
" I suppose you think that that's a gel ? "

Says I ; "may I make so bould as inform ye
That that's a lady ?   Don't let me alarm ye !
But drop this game," I says, "young porpus,
Or I'll lay ye at my feet a corpus—
A corpus."   And then we'd rather a slick
Of roughish water, and I thought she'd be sick,
And that 'd be takin the nonsense out of her ;
But divil-a-bit ! and the saucy pout of her,
And the hair in the wind all flyin away,
And the face all drippin with the spray,
And skippin and trippin, and houldin on,
And many a time I thought she was gone ;
And the joy of the craythur—tumble and toss,
And as fresh as a mackarel, that's what she was.

Aye, and of coorse, you'll see the excuse
This Peter would have for his parley-voos
Them times—for she'd come like a bullet at him,
And he had to catch her, and I had to let him—
And then the slow to cast her adrift,
And the look like some of her was left
In his arms—the divil ! and squeezin there
Agin his breast.   So everywhere,

Blow high, blow low, come smooth or rough,

I'll tell ye what, it was hard enough

For the lot of us to keep them sundered,

Let alone one; for I sometimes wondered

The Captain didn't interfere;

But I fancy he didn seem to see her

Agate of her games; and, if he did,

The terble confidence he had

In me, ye know; and hardly his place

To be watchin, and prowlin, and givin chase

To the leks of these two, that was know'n, no doubt,

When he was likely to be about,

And could aisy dodge him.   But me, you know,

Watch on deck, or watch below,

It's just one watch I had to keep,

Allis at it, and navar no sleep—

Aw bless ye ! navar no sleep at me,

With the freckened, and the 'ziety.[1]

So when we come to the doldhrums, a-lyin

Like a log on the sea, and the paints a-fryin,

And every sowl aboord just done

[1] From being so frightened and anxious.

With the stupid they felt, and the power of the sun—

Lo and behould ! these two was as spruce

As ever—aw well ! it isn no use—

Love it was, I'm parfact willin—

Where won't he go, the little villain !

Hot or could—a despard rambler—

Coast o' Guinea, Novar Zamblar—

"Greenland's icy mountains" the limb !

" India's coral strand," says the hymn ;

Over the hill, and over the hollow,

Like a honey-bee, like a swift, like a swallow,

With the strength and the fire of the sowl that's in him,

Love goes, and will go—who's to pin him ?

Now rael wholesome love, my men,

Will allis have in me a friend—

Love that *is* love—you'll aisy know 't —

Yes, I'm very partial to 't—

Very—it's gettin over me ;

I can't rersist it, don't ye see ?

Can't rersist it, or not much,

Allis takin the part of such.

Aw well, I tell ye, it's surprisin,

I was allis that way, "semperthizin,"
Says a schullar once I was spinnin this twist to 'm,
And had as much grog as was good for his system—
Semperthizin, that's the plan—
Semperthizin, says yandhar man.

So maybe that's the raison he had
The worst lickin of all, but the last, poor lad !
The sun was just down, and a taste of cool
In the air, and the sea was all like gool :
And there I found them sittin aback
Of the cabin companion, and readin a trac',
Or somethin that way.   Aw dear ! I was furious,
Urrov my senses mostly,[1] the curious
It was—for I stood, and I made her rise,
And go, and she went, and the tears in my eyes,
And the click on my heart, and the swim in my brain,
And to force myself against the grain,
And couldn ha' done it, slow or swivel,[2]
If I hadn done it like the divil.

You see, I had to do my duty,

---

[1] Almost out of my senses.　　　　[2] Swiftly.

And, for want of a spur, I got hould of the beauty

Of the chap, for somethin to keep my hard,

And intarmint,[1] you know, that I would regard

For nothin, but welt him, and her navar know'n

What was up, but just to be go'n

To her cabin—And "Is it your beauty, my son?"

I says: "well I'll spile it   that's aisy done—

I'll spile it," I says. "I'll spile it! here goes!"

And I blackened his eyes, and I flattened his nose,

And I mauled him over, every scrap,

Till his mother wouldn ha' known the chap—

Aw boosely, boosely![2] and navar a word

Urrov his mouth—the pluck, good lord!

That *is* the pluck   *Did he strike me?*   No!

Couldn! *in a vice?* just so!

In a vice.   Then I loosed him, and then a dart

Went through me, and I caught him to my heart,

And cried and cried   You'd ha' thought I was drunk

And went and put him in his bunk,

And coaxed him, and nussed him, and washed him
        there,

And made him rather comfibler.

---

[1] Determined.   [2] Beastly, brutally.

Then the fo'c's'le had a meetin,

To see what they'd do, the way I was beatin

Peter; and *wouldn stand it*, they said.

And I went to the meetin, and hung my head

Like a dog, I did. And they grumbled a dale—

Special a chap called Billy Sayle—

But I knew Billy, but—— howavar,

There's people thinks themselves that clavar—

So I said—" Look here ! it's quite correc',

It's only just what I ought to expec',"

I says; " but still you know nothin about it

At all," I says; " so you needn doubt it—

Nothin, no more till brute bases,

And circumstances alters cases."

O yes ! they know'd it all the same,

Says one of the chaps—*Miss What's-her-name*

Had fell in love with Peter, and he

Had fell in love with her, d'ye see ?

And if a gel, no matter the who,

Was fell in love, what's that to you ?

That's for her lover, isn it ?

For him of coorse ! And for me to sit

On the fellow like that—it wasn raison,
No, it wasn ; and talkin amazin—
Talkin, talkin.   " You needn enlarge
On the subjec'," I says : " I takes full charge
Of the case," I says ; "it's all right !
Yes," I says, " I've got a light
About it now," I says : "and Peter
'll know my maenin sooner or later :
And—silence ! my men, now silence ! I say ;
You'll find that's the bettermost way :
I had my orders, you know where from."
Then says Peter- " Go it, Tom !"

So of coorse, you see, I had to do it,
Some way or other to see them through it.
Aw, but I spoke most sirrious [1]
To Peter—aye, the very fuss [2]
I had him by himself : and I found
The lad was sirrious and sound.
Sirrious, and sound, and gud
Aw the rael blood ! the rael blood !
No use o' talkin.   So I swore to him sollum.

---

[1] Seriously.   [2] First (time

On the Bible, of coorse, on the sacred vollum—

I swore if they'd only be true to each other,

And good and that, it's father and mother

And sister and brother they'd find in me—

But "Be cautious!" I says, "whatever there'll be—

Be cautious! and mind the young you are—

And Miss Graeme, of coorse, 'll be meetin her par

All right, and then you'll be tellin him all—

But cautious! cautious! that's the call."

And now for sure [1] I had the trouble,

Double, of coorse—it had to be double—

Them two to look after lek shuperintandin,

Like a father, you know, lek for me to be standin

Betwix them and the Skipper, that he wouldn be knowin

About this coortin that was goin.

Aye, and I had a talk with the two

About it, you know, and what to do,

And the time and the place ; and me to be there

Allis—aw certainly—only fair!

But needn be lookin—at least I could,

---

[1] Indeed.

If I liked : and the book—that was understood—
Navar without the book, no, no !
And readin nice and proper though—
And settled it with them, and Peter chaffin,
And Miss Fanny fit to die with laughin :
But I was dreadful sirrious :
And so, when all was agreed, she bust
A-cryin ; and purty it was to see her ;
And she called me a darlin, and an ould dear
Ould I wasn, not to say—
But still, my goodness ! that's their way.

Well, the book was got, the Bible it was,
My Bible, a splendid Bible, and lost
Betwix them someway ; and tex' for tex',
And clear as a whistle, and all as correck's[1]
A Sunday school.   But then they begun
To change the vesses[2] astonishun
Aw bless ye ! pretendin to read their parts out,
And talkin ! talkin their very hearts out ;
And the eye on the book as stiff as stays,
But coortin reg'lar, and coorted their ways

---

[1] Correct as.   Verses

Through Genesis and Exodus.

And then I gave a bit of a cuss,

And I says—"You'd better be havin a hymn

Now," I says : but just the same—

Slippin in a word on the sly,

Or puttin meanins—navar say die !

And me goin on—but couldn stop it,

And apt to be noticed, and had to drop it.

One day I heard a kiss, and I turned,

And looked at them straight, and their faces burned

With the shame ; and I said—"Just overhaul

The articles," I says, "that's all—

The whole of them—first and second lesson—

Do ! Now was there a word about kissin ?

Now then ? now ? Don't interrup' !

I think I'll have to give it up—

To give the whole thing up ; I'd ax

What else can I do ?" So Miss Fanny made tracks,

But very slow and dignified,

Rather touchy—of coorse, the pride—

Aw pride enough—but navar mind !

But Peter was mad ; and he stayed behind,

And had it out with me there and then—
Aw terble mad he was, to begin—
And if *he* was mad, then so was *I*,
You may depend ; and words got high ;
And he called me this, and he called me that,
And he called me an ould tom-cat --
And—*my heart was hard*, and—*I didn know how*
To behave to a lady, no more till a cow ;
And I hadn no manners, and I hadn no feelins,
And on and on, like priddha[1] peelins.

But at last I gripped him ; and then we agreed
To 'llowance the kisses, and navar exceed
One a sittin ; and me to be present,
But not to be lookin—aw bless ye ! the pleasant
He got, and the quite ;[2] and says he, " What fun !
You're a brick," he says.   But bless ye ! the one
Was made into two, and three, and four,
And half a dozen, and half a score—
Till the tally[3] got mixed lek in general,
And our 'llowancin didn answer at all —
Aw bless ye ! just like bread and butter.

        [1] Potato.   [2] Quiet.   [3] Reckoning.

Glad I was when we got to Calcutta—

And the Colonel and the carriage and pair,

And coachman and footman, all of them there;

And didn know the daughter at all—

No, but had to be—— wh-d'ye-call——

Inthrerjuced? aye, inthrerjuced,

Poor sowl!—aw dear! and her eyes all sluiced

With the tears; and glad enough of the father,

But still—— of coorse, and 'd obvious rather

'a stayed with us—— and—Peter—— when

Was she avar goin to see him again?

And him at the gangway like aside of a grave

She was lowrin into; and then she gave

A look at him, that you'd have thought

All heaven and earth was took and brought

In the one bright flash of love and longing

And forget-me-not, and the people thronging,

And all the row, and all the bother—

That's the last they seen of each other.

Well now, I wouldn trust[1] it'd be runnin

In the teens of years, I was comin to Lunnon

[1] I almost think.

Once from Liverpool, to join a ship,

And, just gettin out o' the train, trip-trip—

And a voice behind me I thought I knew—

"Mr. Baynes, is that you?"

I turned, and, behould ye! there was the woman,

No mistake, but grew uncommon—

Splendid she was—"Miss Fanny Graeme,"

I says, "your sarvint—— is it a dhrame?"

I says; says she—"Just hould your tongue!

You're speakin to Mrs. Peter Young;

And here's my eldest son," says she

And as fine a boy as ever you'd see

"So you married him?" and she nodded her head

"Yes of course."   "Aw dear!" I said.

THE CHRISTENING

Hould him up!
Hould him up!
Joy! joy!
Hould him up! hould him up!
Is that the boy?
Hould him up!

Stand out of the way, women,
Stand out of the way!
Here, Misthress Shimmin!
Here, I say!
Here! here!
Aw dear!
Is this him?
Every limb
Taut and trim—

Here's a hull !
Here's a breast
Like a bull !
He's got my finger in his fess [1]
He hess ! [2] he hess !

Look at the grip !
Is that a smile upon his lip ?
He can't do that !
What ! what !
Smile !
My gough ! what a chile !

Feel the gristle !
Feel it though !
Stop ! I'll whistle
Whew——— ! ho !
What's he doin ?
Is it cooin
You call it when he goes like yandhar ?
See his eyes the way they wandher !
Hullo ! hullo !

[1] Fist.   [2] Has.

Where'll you go? where'll you go?

Keep her so!

There's a look!

There's another!

The little rook!

What's he wantin

With this gallivantin?

Ah! the mother! ah! the mother!

Yiss! yiss! muss hev a kiss!

Aw Kitty, Kitty bogh[1]!

Aw my gough!

Kitty darlin! Kitty then!

And me so far away!

The hard it muss ha' ben![2]

Were you freckened,[3] Kitty, eh?

Navar mind!

Here I am!

As consigned!

And, axin your pardon, Misthress Shimmin,

          ma'am,

Here's the joy!

---

[1] Poor.   [2] Must have been.   [3] Frightened.

Here's our boy, Kitty!
Here's our boy!

Listen! I'll tell you a thing—
By jing!
I've calkerlated it to a dot,
But whether or not—
The very night Kitty was tuk—
Just three days,
If you plaze,
Out of Dantzic, there was a sea struck —
Jemmy 'll remember—
Every timber
Shuck!

Close-hauled, you know, and I navar tould ye,
But behould ye!
In the trough there, rowlin in it,
Just that minute
I saw a baby, as plain,
Passin by on a slant of rain
To leeward, and his little shiff[1]
Streamin away in the long gray drift.

[1] shift.

I saw him there—you didn regard [1] me—

But his face was toward me—

Oughtn't I to know him?

Well, I saw him afore Kitty saw him!

I saw him, and there he ess,[2]

There upon his mother's breast,

The very same, I'll assure ye;

And I think that'll floor ye!

And his body all in a blaze of light—

A dirty night!

"Where was he goin?"

Who's knowin?

He was in a hurry in any case,

And the Baltic is a lonesome place—

But here he is, all right!

Here he is now! joy! joy!

God bless the boy!

Have you tould the Pazon? what did he say?

Has he seen him—ould Pazon Gale?

Aw you tould the Pazon anyway!

Tould! he'll turn the scale

---

[1] See.   [2] Is.

At thirty pound,
I'll be bound.

Did you put it in the papers?
No, no! What capers!
No, no!
Splendid though!
Upon my life-
Catharine, wife
Of Mounseer
Eddard Creer,
Esqueer,
Otherwise dadaa,
Of a son and heer!
Hip-hip-hip-hip, hooraa!

Bless my sowl! am I draemin?
He'll make a seaman
Will yandhar lad—
Aw the glad!
Yiss! yiss! Misthress Shimmin, certainly!
Go down to the smack,
Jemmy, and see-
Yiss! Misthress Shimmin

And all the rest of the women—

'Scuse me, ladies! rather 'cited—

Just the delighted, you know, the delighted!

And every raison to suppose

(See him cockin his nose!)

That the best of care

And ceterar——

I'll get that with Misthress Shimmin—did ye say?

Eh?

Go, Jemmy, they're lyin quite handy,

A bottle of rum and another of brandy,

In the starboard locker theer—

And, Jemmy! there's a taste of gin—

Aw navar fear!

Tell the chaps to finish it—

All the kit—

And listen—tell ould Harper

We'll take and warp her

Inside

On the morning's tide—

About hafe-past four 'll be time to begin—

My gough! but we'll have a chrizzenin!

PEGGY'S WEDDING

" Is that you, Peggy ? my goodness me !

And so dark still I can hardly see !

Wait, woman, wait !

I'll come down ; ye needn go on hommerin at such a rate.

Here's the master snorin

Like a mill, and you to be breakin the door in-—

It's just disthractin, that's what it is—

Aisy, woman ! yis ! yis !—

There's people 'll snore—where's that perricut ?

There's people 'll hommer—my gough ! that slut !

I'm comin ! I'm comin !

God bless the woman !

I navar heard such a row—

    " Aw dear ! aw dear ! aw the craythur ! aw poor Peggy,

        what's the matter with you now ?

Come in ! come in ! the sowl ! the sowl !

What is it, Peggy, what? and where have you left Dan Cowle?

Is he outside in the street?—well, where is he then?

Did you call at the halfway-house? did he get—aw bless
   these men!

Did he fall on the road?   *No*, ye say, *no?*

Well then where did he go?

Is he lyin in the ditch?

Did he lave you, or did you lave him—which?

You left *him?*

So I suppose it's not a man you're wantin at all, but a
   cherubim?

Aye! aye!

Middlin high!

   " And you that were married only yesterday, and the
      weddin out of this house—

To be comin home in the mornin all ragg'd and rumpled
   like a reg'lar trouse [1]—

Peggy, Peggy!   *You'd like to blow the fire, just to feel*

You're at home again—eh, Peggy?   Don't kneel! don't kneel!

Don't be foolish, Peggy.   There! take the bellows,

And blow away!

[1] Slattern.

And we'll have a cup o' tay,

And then you'll tell us.

Why—Dan Cowle! Dan Ballabroo!

A dacent man, and well-to-do!

Dan! Dan Cowle! dear heart!

And the beautiful ye went away in the cart!

And you've tuk and left him! left Dan!

Left the man!"

"*Man!* did ye say? aw Misthriss, Misthriss! what are ye
        talkin?

Man! do ye call that craythur a man, because he's a thing
        that's walkin

On two legs, and a tongue in his head? a beautiful surt [1]

Of a man—you call him a man, I call him a dirt!

That's what I call him—a dirt, and a sneak, and a dunkey—

Man! if that chap's a man, he's a cross twix a man and a
        monkey!

And a touch of a divil, and a touch of a fool—

Listen, Misthriss, listen! We warn half-way up Barrule,

When I thought he'd ha' stayed a bit—and only raisonable
        he shud—

[1] Sort.

At Kinvigs's—bein a thing lek that's general understood—

What's halfway-houses for, I'd like to know—

Just so !

You wouldn be agen [1] that ?

What ?

 "Certainly ! and company waitin—and just a drop to
  warm a body—

And dear me ! what is there in half a glass of rum, or a
  whole glass, for the matter of that, to harm a body ?

And well you know it isn the dhrink I regard—

Well you know that—but still a body's hardly prepar'd

To pass the only public-house on the road drivin home on
  your weddin night—

It isn right,

Nor correck, nor friendly, nor in any surt of a concatenation

Lek accordin to your station—

And disappintin people that way, when they're trustin

Your proper feelins, is quite disgustin.

 "So I lays my hand on his arm, just by way of signifyin—

Nothin more—and behould ye ! he cocks hisself up as stiff
  and as dignifyin,

<hr>

[1] Against.

And rip! and rup! and chip! and chup!

And 'There's nobody up,' he says: nobody up!

And glasses jinglin, and windows blazin,

And people comin out, and shoutin amazin

To stop—but no! but sticks his elbers like skewers in a
    body—

'What!' I says, 'not a glass of toddy?

Just for neighbourly dacency?'

'It's surprisin how early they're goin to bed,' says he.

'Goin to bed!' says I. 'Yes,' he says—middlin snarly—

'Kinvigs's was allis early,' he says, 'partic'lar early'

And his ould hoss gallopin, and heisin his hindquarters,
    and workin

Like a see-saw, and bumpin and jerkin,

And sent me flyin, with my head in the bottom of the cart,
    and my feet in the air,

And the rest of me—anywhere.

  "So he puts out his hand

'Bless my sowl!' he says, 'I thought it was gone!'

'What?' says I. 'The box,' he says, maenin my box, and
    my weddin bonnet

Smashed to jammy 'I wish you'd sit upon it,'

He says—the box, of coorse. So I thought I'd be a little
  lovin

And that—and I comes up lek gradjal, lek shiftin and shovin

Lek agen him in a way. And I says, 'I'd like to be with
  you,' says I,

' My own husband,' I says ; for I thought it better to try

Was there just a taste

Of anything of a husband in him : so he put his arm round
  my waist—

Not round either—for he couldn do that—

Not for the stout I am, bein allis a gintale figger, but just
  like a lath,

Flat

Agen the back o' my stays, and not the smallest curl

Or squeeze in the ould pump-handle, not the smallest in the
  worl'—

"And his eyes on the box—and 'There it's goin !'

He says, and wacin and woin—

And as restless. And then we got on the mountain ; and
  the ling

Was smellin very sweet in the dark, and a stream began
  ting-ting-ting

Down the other way—very pleasant, and it got couldher,

And I thought it was only a 'spectable thing to put my head

    on his shouldher.

  "Oh dear! he got as crabbit

As an ould buck rabbit;

And he hitched and he hunched, and he cribbed and he

    crunched,

Till he was all bunched

In a lump; and anyway his blades that sharp

And snaggy you might as well ha' leaned your head on the

    backbone of a carp.

  "So I didn care, and I sat up as straight

And as indepandin. It was gettin late

When we come to his house: and there was a falla theer

    standin on the look-out

On the very top of the midden, and jumps down, and grips

    the hoss, and gives a big shout,

And 'Look here!' he says, 'who's goin to pay me?'

    'Pay!'

Thinks I—and this ould fool goin seerchin away

In all his pockets and gev a start,

And 'Bless my heart!'

He says, 'hev I lost it? hev I lost it?' and twisses and
wriggles

Hisself into knots—and the other chap stands and sniggles—

A young chap—And 'Dear me!' says Dan, 'it must ha'
dropt out on the road comin—

It's very disthressin,' he says. 'Faith then! you're a
rummin,'

Says the chap, and like to buss [1]—

'What's the use o' talkin?' says Dan Cowle, 'I've lost my
puss.

Where's your puss, Peggy? maybe,' he says, 'you'll not
mind

Payin the man,' he says—'if you'll be so kind,'

He says—but oh! that creepin, and that sneakin, and that
slewin and that screwin,

Like a conger just. And 'What's a doin?'

Says I; 'isn it your own cart you got?'

'Well—— no—— it's not,'

He says, 'I must confess—

The fact of the matter is,' he says,

'My own cart is bruk very bad,

[1] Burst.

And I borrowed this one for the occasion.'   So I paid the
    lad.

   "'Aye, aye! his cart is bruk very bad,' says the chap,
'Likewise his trap,
And the phaeton, and the barooch, and the jantin-car, and
    the family coach-and-four'—
And he gev a roor
Out of hisself, this young divil—
And 'Hurrah for the weddiners!' he says.   'Be civil! be
    civil!'
Says Dan, 'be civil, young man, it would well become ye' —
But says I —'Take your money and your cart,' I says, 'and
    be off with ye, ye scum ye!
Be off!' I says, 'stir your stumps!'
(These Foxdale lumps [1]
Is pirriful.[2])   And Dan with the box on the street, and pokin
The key in the door—and, you know, I seen the chimbley
    wasn smokin
Nor nothin nor no cowhouse about that I could see,
Nor no garden, nor a bush, let alone a tree—
But just a crock

---

   [1] Lads.   [2] Pitiful, detestable.

Standin on a rock,

And water runnin in it very free

At the gable, and slishin and slushin, and muckin the street

Under one's feet.

" And this is the man that tould me he'd make me

So comfible !

But still

You'll not mistake me,

You know me, Misthriss, don't ye? and you know I wouldn

   .   flinch,

No, not even if I was deceived—no, not an inch ;

On I'd go, through the smooth and the rough,

Content enough—

For richer for poorer, for better for wuss—

Lost his puss !

Had he ? lost two ! lost twenty !

Give me a man with a lovin heart, Misthriss, with a lovin

      heart—

That's plenty—

Plenty for me—navar mind the cart—

With a lovin heart, and some wit about him—

And I'd navar doubt him

Misthriss—no! *for better for wuss*—

Them's the words, and didn the Pazon say them?   And
      I'd nuss

His childher, and I'd work, and I'd slave, and I'd die

Before I'd be beat—and still a lie

Is a dirty thing—fore or aft,

As the sailors is sayin—

But listen again—

Misthriss! Misthriss! you don't know half.

   "So we got in, however, and he groped about, and he
      found a flint-and-steel,

And he skinned his ould knuckles all like a priddha[1] peel,

Streck-streckin away ; and, when he gor[2] a light at last,

You navar seen such a rookery—a dresser there was—

Yis—but hardly a plate or a bason, or any other surt o' war',

And a hape of mouldy turmits[3] in a corner there—could,
      comfortless things they are

And a rot-hole,[4] or a shot-hole, I don't know which, and I
      don't care etha',[5]

And a barrel that looked like male, with a flag or a slate
      on the top of it, and a medha,[6]

---

[1] Potato.   [2] Got.   [3] Turnips.   [4] Rat-hole.
    [5] Either.   [6] Small, one-handled tub.

And a pot, and nothin in it, and no fire, if there had been,
    and as for bed or beddin—
Well, I dedn throuble, no, faith, I dedn.

"It was a house that if you were inside you'd see about
    as much sky as roof,
A surt o' mixthar o' the two, and a touch of harry-long-
    legses and spiders—aw, it's the troof![1] it's the troof,
The troof I'm tellin; and the scraas[2] hangin in rags and
    strings of dirt as black
You couldn tell were they scraas, or strips tore from a
    rotten ould sack,
Or nettin or somethin. And I can tell ye the chap begun,
    as a body might say,
To look rather ashamed of hisself—I think so—in a way—
Yis—he didn look at me for a bit at all,
But cocked his face agen the wall.

"And—'It's too late,' he says, 'it's too late for supper, I
    suppose '—
And ye might have sniffed and sniffed till ye straint your
    nose
Afore you'd ha' got a smell of supper in yandhar place—

---

[1] Truth.   [2] Strips of sod laid on the rafters under the thatch.

But he turned at last, and I saw his face—

Workin, workin, workin most terrible,

And screwin the eye, and workin still—

And—'Let's sit down a bit,' he says, and he studdied the
        candle, if ye plaze, and he looks up as innocent as a
        linnet,

And he says, 'That's a nice puss you've got,' he says; 'how
        much is there in it?'

And I tould him £4 : 16s. and 2½d. farlin—

So he says, 'That's a nice little bit o' money, my darlin—

Let's see it,' he says.

                        So I gev it to him, ye know;

And he counted it out, I tell ye, every coin of it, very
        slow—

Very slow he counted—and then—what d'ye think?

Whips it in his pocket!   'A nice lump of jink!'

Says Dan; and he snuggled up closer to me, and he began
        to fiddle and fiddle,

Lek tryin to span me round the middle—

Some surt o' coortin? thinks I, *he's improvin, I doubt*—

The ould villyan! he was just tryin to find out

Had I any more stitched up in my stays!

And a man with such ways—

Would you call him a man? now would ye, Misthriss?
    would ye, though?
That was the fiddlin—aye! he said it, he said it hisself, the
    ould crow!
Yis, and his dirty ould mouth all of a pucker, and grippin
    and nippin,
And declarin he felt the shillins slippin
Between the quiltins—aw dear! aw dear!
But I was enough for him—navar fear!

    "I says—'This is no place for me,' I says; and up I
        jumps—
'I'm off,' I says; and he rattles his ould stumps—
And—'Off?' he says—'why you've not opened your
    box yet!'
'Clear out o' the road!' I says. 'I hevn seen your
    frocks yet,'
He says, 'nor the sheetin nor nothin!—just give us that
    key—
It's every bit my proppity!' he says. 'Out o' the way!'
I says, and I gript the box. But if I gript it, he gript it,
    and he shouted and bawled,
And backards and forrards we tugged and we hauled;

And we staggered this way, and we staggered that way,

And higgledy-piggledy, and I cannot tell what way—

But I gev him a run in on the dresser, and his ould back bent,

And—— down he went!

  "And the crockery—what there was—all smashed—well
     to be sure!

And the turmits rowlin on the floor—

So the box was mine, and I out on the door.

'Murdher! tieves!' and he run after me full trot—

'You're a robber!' he says; 'you've robbed me! every-
     thing you got

Belongs to me—I'll bring a shuit,' he says, 'I'll bring a shuit

For damagers!' he says—the ould brute—

'I'll have your life!' he says,

'Ar'n you my wife?' he says—

'Murdher!' he says, 'murdher!'   '*Murdher*—your granny,'

I says—'Good-bye, Dan Cowle! good-bye, Danny!'

And I left him standin in the road; and here I am, as you
     see—

And, Misthriss! no more weddins, aw good sakes! no
     more weddins for me!"

MARY QUAYLE

The Curate's Story

We went to climb Barrule,
Wind light, air cool—
But when we reached the crest
That fronts Cornaa,
A black cloud leaned its breast
Upon the bay—
And, seeing from Ayre to Maughold Head
The long wings spread
Slumb'rous with brazen light,
Swift dropping from the height
We follow
The crags that northward shoot,
And find ourselves within the hollow
Of Gob-ny-Scuit—

o

Spout-mouth—so named because
It seems as if a giant's jaws
Gaped wide—
Ent'ring, we lay down side by side.

   Then Richard said-
" This is the place—
Long years have fled ;
But still I see her face.
Just here where you are she was—yes, just here—
I had long thought she loved me ; but you know the fear--
Had thought,—but now by what sweet word made bolder
I cannot tell ;
Only her dear head fell
Upon my shoulder,
And she looked up into my eyes—and this
Was our first kiss."

   As Richard spoke, from out that awful cloud
The lightning leaped, and loud
The boom
Of the long thunder thrilled the deep'ning gloom.
Then Richard spoke again   " That very day

Next year I came this way,

But it was different :

Yes, God had sent

A trial that was hard to bear ;

And so I went,

And took my care

Up to these hills,

Alone, alone !

And knelt, and prayed to Him who bends our wills,

And can subdue them to His own—

" For Mary . . . Mary [Oh how the lightning flashed !

Oh how the thunder crashed !]

Die? No, she did not die—I thought you knew—

Sir, Mary was not true. . . .

Yes, sir, I will be patient—you shall see—

Patient—O certainly—

Patient—God knows I am ; God knows I've need to be.

" Mary was ruined, sir ;

She bore a child that was not mine—

Nay, do not stir—

The lightning, is it ? Sir, we may resign

What's ours, if so we make it happier;
But oh! to see it in the dust,
Down-trodden, broken —
Aye, and by one in whom you had full trust,
Stained and defiled,
This is the grief that never can be spoken—

"This was my grief. The father of her child
Was a young gentleman, who came to spend
A summer in the Island. Truest friend
He seemed to me—he had such hearty ways
With men like us. It was his holidays
At Oxford College—that's where scholars go
To learn for clergymen—but, sir, you know —
You were at Oxford —well, well, never mind—
I loved the lad, so gentle and so kind
He was; and fond enough he seemed of me,
And always wishing for my company.

"So he and I were friends, and took delight
In one another. Hadn't we the right?
And yet he never knew that Mary Quayle
Was anything to me. To hand the sail,

To steer, to haul, he would himself devote;

We never talked of sweethearts in the boat.

He wasn't much account when he began,

But came to be a splendid fisherman—

I taught him everything, except to swim—

He beat me there; and I was fond of him.

" The days were short, the leaves were thin and brown,

When Mr. Herbert Dynely left the town.

I rowed him to the steamer: when we fetched,

He jumped upon the paddle-box, and stretched

His hand for mine, and would not let it go—

'God bless you, Dick!' he cried; 'I hardly know

If ever I shall see your face again.'

And looked and looked. I thought the very strain

Of truth was in his eye; and so I yearned

To him, and could not speak. But, if I'd turned,

I might have seen a window where a face

As white as death was glued against the glass—

Long after, when the talk was everywhere,

Some people told me who had seen her there.

It was an early sailing, and the sun

Shot in upon her, level like a gun—

And they saw her—

God in heaven !

(Forgiven ! yes, forgiven !

But saw her.)

Stupid, half-naked, so they said,

Sprung from her bed,

Her breast

All pressed,

Crushed, murdered, on the sill,

Like a woman that's not respectable.

"No. I knew nothing all the time ; nor after,

For many a week—I've sat with her, and chaffed her

Because she was more silent than she used;

And yet she never looked a bit confused,

But sweet and gentle as a girl could be,

So sweet and gentle still she was to me.

Indeed, I think that she looked happier

Than ever she had done—I saw in her

A deeper joy ; so that our love would seem

Sometimes a dream within another dream.

"And so it was : and what the dreaming meant

I had no thought, and I was quite content.

I looked into her eyes, and saw as far

As made me happy—that's the way we are—

A swimmer tips the tangles, can he know

The depth of water that there's down below?

I don't complain. I'm sure she loved me; yes—

The greater love had swallowed up the less.

"But still she loved me. Ah, sir! who was I?

A candle, when the sun is in the sky,

Is hardly noticed—did the night, no doubt;

But now you even forget to put it out.

He was that sun that rose in heav'n above,

And burst upon her in a blaze of love.

Poor candle! steady, burning to the snuff—

I know our love is only common stuff.

It's faithful as the mothers were that bore us;

It's just the love our fathers loved before us.

There's nothing fine about it, nothing grand,

Like fruit or flower that comes from foreign land:

A clover blossom where the bumbees cling,

And suck—that's all; you know the sort of thing.

A blackbird to his mate pipes nothing strange,

A sweet old tune, that has not any change.
So we, when we have told our love, are fain
To take a kiss, and tell it all again.
But true it is, the love no power can sunder,
The strongest love, is love whose root is wonder.

" And Dynely was a wonder over here,
Especially with women—far or near
You would not see his match—so generous
And free, and then so different from us—
His talk, his clothes, his way with every limb-
We hadn't any chance at all with him.
Ah, sir ! compared with such a common clod
As me, this Dynely looked a perfect god
There's nothing like it since the world began,
The beauty of a noble Englishman.

" And Dynely was no flirt, no butterfly,
That's always on the wing : he didn't try
To get the girls to gather all around him—
But rather serious in his ways I found him.
And when she came to know that she was dear
To such a man, poor Mary had no fear,

But only wonder : so that, when the crest

Of that great wave of love rose to her breast,

She floated off her feet, and drifted out

Into love's deep-sea soundings : no faint doubt

Was in her mind ; through all the depths she clung

To that strong swimmer's arm ; and, as he flung

Around her all the glory of his youth,

He seemed to her the very soul of truth.

" Ah, sir ! it was a way with perils fraught,

If she had thought ; but love is not a thought.

What thought she had was only that he'd take her

To some bright land of joy, where he would make her

His queen, his . . . God-knows-what . . . some fruitful
        land,

Where happiness would grow at his command,

Like grass in fields, and none their joys should sever,

And all her soul be satisfied for ever.

I see you understand—the reason why

Is plain—ah, who was I, sir ? who was I ?

" And yet . . . there's something bothering my brain—

Just wait a bit—I'll make my meaning plain.

You see, I've not the art you scholars learn
To find the very word for every turn
Of what you think, and feel within your heart,
Immediately—ah, sir! that *is* an art!
But this is it—you'll see it at a glance—
The man that paints a picture has a chance
To make it what he likes—he'll paint the trees,
He'll paint a baby on its mother's knees.
He paints the things that give him most delight,
He paints the things he longs for in the night,
And things that never were, and never could be,
He paints them up to what he thinks they should be—
What's this you call—imagination, ain't it?
Why, every yearning of his heart, he'll paint it.
He'll paint the very life, and make it start out
Straight in your face—the man can paint his heart out.
He's safe enough; and yet he needn't brag—
It's all between him and a canvas rag.

     " And so you gentlemen that write the po'ms
And stories, living in your pleasant homes
You're not content with just the things you see
Around you, common joy and misery,

And life and death.   You set yourselves to listen
To all the hearts that beat ; all eyes that glisten,
No matter where, you watch, you watch the faces ;
You write as if you lived in fearful places,
So that, at times, your best friends wouldn't swear
You are the steady gentlemen you are.

"All right ! all right again—no fear of you :
But only tell me what are we to do !
We also have our dreams—be sure of that :
We also long, we hardly know for what.
God floods our hearts with all His melting snow,
And there's no sluice to take the overflow.
And so it often happens that the mill
Is swept away, or broken.   You have skill
Of books and paints for what your mind contrives ;
But we can only put it in our lives.
There's many a poor man's daughter born with wings
Inside, that fret upon her heart like stings,
Till some one comes at last, and stands, and breathes
Upon the wings.   Then from their golden sheaths
They flash into the light : with some of us
It's very hard indeed ; it's dangerous.

" But when poor Mary could not hide her shame,
And had to speak, it was her mother came
And told me all.   At first, it hardened me—
But, sir, it was a common misery—
And who'd be more heart-broken than the mother?
And so we tried to comfort one another.
The father was a fine old Methodist—
They said, when he was told, he clenched his fist,
And trembled like a leaf, and bowed his head :
But, when he raised it up again, they said
It was a sad, but still a lovely sight
The old man's face was full of heavenly light.

" Yes, real pious Methodists they were :
And that's what made it harder still to bear
Being so much looked up to in the place—
It was a very terrible disgrace.
But, Methodists or not, we know who sends
The troubles ; and, except amongst our friends,
That know us best, we have not much to say
We suffer, and are silent   that's our way.
The women, too, with us, are very meek
Poor souls ! it isn't for revenge they seek,

Or law, or money.   Love is what they sought ;

And, if that's gone, then all the world is nought.

Revenge ?   That's not the port for which they sailed—

For love they ventured, and for love they failed :

And so they'd like to die, if we would let them :

And all they ask is just that we'd forget them.

   " But, when her time was come, the mother sent

For me, and so I forced myself, and went ;

And stayed a while outside, and listened there,

And heard the preacher putting up a prayer,

And heard a long low moaning in the garret—

You know what that was, sir—I could not bear it.

And when I saw a woman coming out

Upon the landing—well, I turned about,

And started home.   But, somewhere near the mill,

I heard a step behind me—it was Phil,

Her oldest brother—she had three—

Fine fellows as could be, . . .

And she . . .

Was their joy and their pride . . .

Any one of them would have died

In a minute for her. . . . They loved to see her

So good, and so sweet ;

And so she was, my darling, darling dear !

She was ! she was ! before this awful wreck—

And Philip took me round the neck,

And kissed me on the street,

And off without a word .

Mary ! Mary !

I feel her in my arms . .

Her mouth warms . . .

Yes then ! press then !

Where then ?   There then !

Mary ! Mary ! . . .

The very ground she trod

My God ! "

[Oh how the lightning flashed '

Oh how the thunder crashed !]

Richard fell back, and would have struck his head

Against the rock ; but I my arms outspread,

And caught him as he fell.   He could not speak,

Scarce breathe.   I raised him up, and stroked his
        cheek,

And cherished him, till, from the viewless bourn

Of death, the anguished spirit made return.

Then Richard spoke—

     " I know that you must wonder

How Mary's brothers could be patient under

Such wrong, and such disgrace : perhaps you thought

They'd kill the man ; perhaps you think they ought.

Well—that is not our way. Moreover, sir,

The lads were thinking not of him, but her.

They hadn't backed him, and they hadn't crossed him ;

They hadn't loved him, and they hadn't lost him.

And now they could not hate him. He was just

A reef that they had split upon ; a gust

Of strong and terrible wind, that had capsized

The ship in which they'd stored what most they prized—

Or as the lightning there, that stoops, and kills,

And passes—vanishing behind the hills—

Who's angry with the lightning ?

       Even so

They never talked of Dynely as a foe,

Nor talked of him at all ; but gathered round

Their sister in her sorrow—every sound

And every sight they thought would aggravate

Her trouble they would screen her from, and wait

And watch like three big dogs, and keep a ring

Of love and peace about her.   Everything
They could they did : and when they saw her tearful—
Poor chaps ! they'd try to be a little cheerful :
And, when they could do nothing else, they'd sit
With her, and leave off talking for a bit,
And be a comfort to her—three of a size,
All pitying her with those big loving eyes.

" She was the loveliest thing they'd ever known :
She was the youngest of them ; she had grown
Among them like a flower among the corn—
So, from the very minute she was born,
They loved their little sister.   And to them
The flower that drooped, and faded on the stem,
Was still their flower : the lightning-flash had scathed it,
And scorched the tender leaves ; and so they bathed it
With dews of love, and every sweet endeavour—
She was as beautiful to them as ever,
And twice more precious for her sorrow's need -
So God is gentle to the bruised reed.
Besides, they hoped for sunshine by and by,
If only they could coax her not to die.
No score but Time will wipe it with his sponge –

Too much to lose, they thought : so divers think, and
    plunge.

" I wandered all that night upon the shore ;

But, when the day broke, I was at the door

Again ; and Philip told me that her child

Was born, and Mary seemed quite reconciled

To nurse it, and they both would live.   I knew

That very minute what I had to do.

The packet sailed for Liverpool that day,

And I sailed with her.   Yes, sir, as you say,

To speak to Mr. Dynely, if I could,

And bring him home to Mary—God was good

That had preserved her, and I thought he might

Do *his* part now, and come and make all right.

" I was most wretched, sir, aboard that craft—

Some chaps are very thoughtless ;—and they chaffed

And bothered me.   They're very different now

From fishermen like us : I don't know how,

But quite another sort—they hardly seem

Like sailors—maybe something in the steam.

But Corlett, that was skipper of the boat

(A better seaman never was afloat),
Reproved them very sharp, and made them cease
Their stuff, and then I got a little peace.

 "I landed at the Stage, and looked about,
And hailed a Runcorn flat, just clearing out,
And jumped aboard : the skipper gave a curse ;
His wife looked up, and asked if I could nurse,
And handed me the baby ; so I sat,
And nursed a baby on a Runcorn flat
And glad enough—God knows that I had need
Of something innocent ; I had indeed -
Poor little things !   But when the night came on,
And all the stars, the woman nursed her son,
And talked to me of heaven, and of another
That she had lost, a little baby brother—
And how *the world was full of sin and care—
But God was all, and God was everywhere*
I told her nothing ; but of course she knew
Far more than half my . . . Well, you know, they do
A woman has an art you'll never shirk,
She always knows another woman's work.

 "At Runcorn, when I asked for Dynely Hall,

The only bearings I could get at all
Were just south-east; and so I bore away;
And, on the morning of the second day,
I saw the place before me.   Aren't they grand?—
Those big old houses rooted deep in land;
And woods and park that stretch for miles and miles,
And meadows like long lakes of grass, and stiles,
And paths—and all so open and so free—
Ah, what's our Milntown, and our Nunnery,
Or Bishop's Court?   Just think—the room alone—
No cropping every acre to the bone,
Like us.   There's money at the back—that's it!
Yes, money: but there's more; there's noble wit,
There's ancient memories, use of generous ways,
And wholesome customs of the bygone days.

   " So when I saw the glory and the strength
Of such a place, and when I saw the length
Of roofs, and spires, and gable-ends, and towers,
And high stone-windows cut in fruits and flowers—
And grass like thick-napped velvet on the lawn,
And all so quiet sleeping in the dawn—
I thought two thoughts—What right had I to bring

My trouble *there?* and then—What earthly thing
Could make it possible for Mary Quayle
To be the mistress there?—could love prevail?
Could honesty? . . . And then I stood uncertain,
Upon the stretch, as one who holds the curtain
Of some sound sleeper, knowing that he never
Will sleep like that again. And then a shiver
Came over me—a long dim driving scud
Of horror, and my eyes were burning blood,
And the world rose around me, and I fell
Forward . . . down to the very bottom of hell.

"Then from the pit I cried a bitter cry—
The pit indeed—I swore to God on high
This thing was wrong, and always must be wrong—
I swore it in the darkness: then . . . ding-dong .
The blood-bells bubbled in my ears like rain,
And earth and sky came back to me again ;
And I was on my knees upon the sod,
And praying ; and I said

      'O God, my God !
Thou art the Father of all souls : from Thee
They come, as equally ordained to be

The creatures of Thy hand, Thy sovereign might,
And they are equal, Father, in Thy sight.
O God! my God! in that sweet field of morn,
Where all the souls were waiting to be born,
Were they not equal? and, if not so now,
Who makes these differences? God, not Thou!
Not Thou! not Thou, my God! And love is Thine;
Thou pourest it into our hearts like wine
In golden cups; and Love is just the same
As Thou art, God: he knows no rank, or name,
Or wealth, or place. He takes our hearts and binds
    them
With links of fire—Oh, say not that he blinds them
With vain deceits! not *that*, O Heavenly Father!
Not that, not that! if truth is truth: say rather—
Wise Love comes opening our eyes to see
The stamp of natural equality.
O Lord, I pray Thee, let these two be one,
And as for me, O Lord, Thy will be done!
I will not say a word, a single word—
Thy will be done! Thy will be done, O Lord!
I loved her—yes—perhaps I loved her most—
It might have been—O Lord, O Lord, Thou know'st.

And now be with me in this dreadful hour;

Subdue the pride of man, and give me power

To sacrifice myself right out and through —

This much I ask, O Lord, this much I do.

O Lord, I claim to have no part or lot

In her; I only ask to be forgot.

Make these two happy in their love, and then—

I'll manage—grant it, God of love! Amen!'

[No more the lightning flashed,

No more the thunder crashed—

But from the piléd jet

Gleamed sheeted violet,

Which lent such grace

To that sad face,

My voice was all to seek:

And when I tried to speak, I could not speak.

Then Richard smiled to see how absolute

The human tie that bound us blessed fruit

Of strong coequal manhood. Then he spoke]

" Day strengthened [Richard said]; I saw the smoke

Rise from the roofs: the birds began their hymns,

And all the valley seemed to stretch its limbs,

And wake.   It was a lovely spot ; and so

I felt a great deal better,—cheerful—no—

But better ; thinking God had heard my prayer,

And everything so pleasant and so fair.

And then, for coolness like, and also knowing

Where *he* would be, if there was fishing going,

I went and sat me down upon the brink

Of a fine stream, that had a merry blink,

And looked, so clear and quick the water ran,

Like our own rivers in the Isle of Man.

The sound was sweet, the wind came off the moor,

I might have been in Sulby, or Ballure.

" Then sleep came on me, and I dreamt a dream

Of Mary skipping to me 'cross the stream

Upon some stepping-stones ; and I was standing

With arms stretched out to catch her at the landing :

And her sweet face was just a perfect sun

Of love and mischief.   Suddenly—' Run, run ! '

She cried, ' the child ! '   I looked, and all was dark,

Only I saw a little baby stark

Naked as it was born, and over it

I saw a ball of rosy flame that lit

Its little body, as it floated there—
I felt the night-wind whistling through my hair—
I saw poor Mary leap—I sprang to hold her—
I woke—and . . . Dynely's hand was on my shoulder.

   "'Why, Richard, Richard! what on earth is this?
And what is up? and what has gone amiss?
And how in Heaven's name have you come here,
My lusty, trusty, Ancient Mariner!
Ha! Richard, you've been spreeing—that's your line!
You've been among the landsharks, Richard mine.
You steady chaps are far the worst, they say,
When once you cut the cable.' Just his way—
Landsharks, and *Ancient Mariners*, and that :
And gript my arm, and held my hand, and sat
Beside me.
        But I turned away my head,
And . . . 'Sir, the child is born, the child,' I said.
He dropt me, gript me, dropt and gript again—
Gript like a vice; and . . . ' Richard! Richard Craine,'
He said— 'Look here! look straight! look straight!' and
     turned me
Around to look at him full front, and burned me

With eyes like coals of fire—'Look straight!' says he;

'There's something in your face I want to see—

You loved her, Craine!' I gave him look for look—

Ah sir, the murdering devil has a nook

In every heart—another move, a breath—

I might have had him in the grips of death—

Die him, die me, or die the two of us—

What matters it? The thing is thus and thus—

It's come to *that*—you don't know how or why—

You don't know anything—— oh d—— you! die!

"Die—— yes—but Mary—— Mary was the thing:

And why was I at Dynely but to bring

That man to do the duty of a lover,

And come and make an honest woman of her?

And who was I to put between them? No!

Just let me see her happy, and I'd go,

And never more be heard of, never more—

You *can* do *that*. 'You loved her, Craine.' I swore

I never did . . . I had to do it . . . yes . . .

I had—God knows the lie; but, nevertheless,

There was no other way in heaven above

Or earth beneath—it was the lie of love.

"I said that we were friends—that Mary's father
And mine had been old shipmates—that they rather
Had trust in me, and thought that I could tell
Their grief to him, through knowing him so well—
So I had come : and *Mary was as pure
As the unmelted snow*, I said : *he knew her,*
I said—*she was a modest woman still,
And all her people were respectable.*
I said a lot of things : but then a cloud
Came on his handsome face, and he looked proud
And cold at me : again the devil hissed
Hot murder in my heart.   I held his wrist—
It felt like paper, cracking in my span

"And—'Mr. Dynely, you're a gentleman.'
I said, 'and so our girls are only toys
For you to play with, slaves of lustful joys
To you, and such as you, that you may break them
For fun and fancy—eh ? that you may make them
A desolation, and a shame to utter,
And fling them on the cinders or the gutter,
As children fling their dolls : and we must stand
Patient   we, fathers, brothers—move no hand

To right the wrong.   It *is* a wrong ! what rule ?

What law is this ? who made it ? God ?   That's cool !

What God ? whose God ? the God of heaven and earth ?

The God that brings all creatures to the birth ?

The God Eve prayed to when she suckled Cain,

And Adam saw the milk ?   Your god is plain,

The devil-god, that made him kill his brother,

The god that sunders us from one another

In jealousy and hate, friend torn from friend—

In murder it began, in murder it will end.'

" My grip grew tighter—' God, and law ! ' I cried :

' Your god is Moloch, and your law is pride—

Hell's pride ; man's law—man therefore can reverse it—

Stand up with me, I say, and curse it ! curse it !

Curse it !· it is no part of God's great plan—

A gentleman ! stand up, and be a man ! '

[While Richard paused, as if the passionate speech

Had overmastered utterance—lo ! a breach

Of purest sky, seaward, diagonal

From north to south ; on either side, a wall

Black, feather-edged with sheen of silvery bars,

And in the interspace were many stars.
I saw it, but was silent.   Richard broke
A way for prisoned words, and thus he spoke—]

"If I had not been blind with grief and passion,
I could not but have noticed how the fashion
Of Dynely's face was changing all the while—
But now I saw it—saw the sweet bright smile
Spread out through tears ; and—'Richard Craine,' he said,
'I come on Friday.'   Then I fell stone dead—
You see, the tramping, and the want of meat,
And all—I just fell senseless at his feet.

"He raised me though, and made me take a sup
Of brandy from a little silver cup
He had with him, and gave me food he'd brought
For fishing store : and then, like losing thought
Of all our cares, as, when a storm has passed,
Two vessels, hull to hull, and mast to mast,
Lie on the heaving calm   just so we lay,
And talked chance talk   of herrings in the bay,
And six-foot congers *did I catch them often?*
There's men would talk of congers in their coffin

Chance talk, chance talk—that's it, and very much

Like dropping stones in water . . . touch-touch-touch—

That's all—and so I said I thought I'd hook it :

And Dynely gave me money, and I took it—

I did—you see, I didn't want to lose

A minute getting home, and to refuse

Seemed foolish pride ; and, on the other hand,

To take—— but, sir, I see you understand.

" He showed me where the railway ran aback

The hills.   I said good-bye, and didn't slack

Until I reached the level—then I stopped,

And saw him stretched upon his face arm-propped,

Arm-buried from the world of living men—

Ah sir, I could have ripped my heart out then,

And flung it back to him—' He's good ! he's good !'

I cried, and turned, and sprang into the wood.

Thank God that that last moment I had grace

And power to see that Dynely was not base,

To feel that he was good, sound at the core—

Because . . . because . . . I never saw him more !

" How sweet the night is getting ! [Then said I—

'It is a lovely night'—whereat a sigh
Came trembling to our feet, then paused, as failing
Against the rock, then fluttered into wailing,
And wheeled adown the farthest bourn of west—
'The thunder-wind is dying in its nest,'
Said Richard : but I knew not what to think,
So human was the sorrow, to the brink
Of syllabled utterance urging awful cares—
I followed it with wishes and with prayers.
Then Richard said—]

" The boat was late, the evening air was cool,
The sun's last light was creeping up Barrule ;
The place looked very happy, very sweet ;—
And I was happy.   Up Kirk Maughold Street
I met the brothers.   Heavy with distress,
They looked at me : but all I said was ' Yes,
He's coming ;' for they knew where I had gone—
I saw they did   they nodded, and passed on,
Suspicious, whispering, or seemed to be,
And all the people stood and stared at me.

" But I went up to Mary's.   Mrs. Quayle

Was standing at the door : I told my tale—

She couldn't speak, she hardly raised her head,

But fell against the door—'Come in,' she said.

Old Quayle had got the preacher, Mr. King,

A Bible gript between them arguing ;

And, just as I was standing at the sill,

The preacher snatched the Bible from him, till

He'd find a text to pin him.   Low, quite low,

Says Mrs. Quayle, 'He's seen him—*him*, you know.'

The Bible straddled somewhere in their laps,

Old Quayle heaved back his head, and sighed ; perhaps

It was the waking up of all the grief

Had slept awhile, perhaps it was relief

From preachers' talk, because there are, no doubt,

Some preachers that you'd rather do without,

When you're in trouble ; and old Quayle was all

For peace and holy joy, like John, like Paul,

For quietness, and prayer, and meditation—

Though Paul—— I think—— but smelling provocation

Was King's delight ; but still I've understood

He was a man that did a deal of good.

" And now I told them what I'd seen and heard,

How I had met with Dynely—every word
He'd said to me; but not, of course, what I
Had said; and Mrs. Quayle began to cry.
But all the time that I was speaking there,
I saw the preacher working in his chair,
And now a sniff, and now a snuff – 'I know,'
He seemed to say, 'what you're a-coming to.'
And when I told how Dynely had agreed
To come next boat —'Indeed,' he said, 'indeed!'—
And sniffed.   But now an argument began
Between himself and Mrs. Quayle—*What plan,*
He said, *should be adopted in this case*
And—*how astonishing it was to trace*
The hand of Providence ; how human ill
Was overruled for good ;—unsearchable,
The preacher said, *it was, past finding out,*
Like all God's ways.   See how He'd brought about
A full conviction ! see the sinner's sin
A cause of grace ! but not to walk therein —
He said —*No, no ! And Mary's change was deep,*
He said, *and highly promising   a sheep,*
He doubted not, brought home upon the shoulder
Of the Good Shepherd.   Now then, if they told her

About this Dynely, where was all his wrestling?

This work would be disturbed, this lamb, a-nestling

Upon the Saviour's bosom, would give ear

To wolves without the fold ; and so, one dear

To him by precious ties would fall away ;

And God would question at the Judgment Day.

" Poor Mrs. Quayle had not the slightest chance

With King—indeed, she hardly made advance

Beyond some simple words, like—'Surely ! surely !

They're better married.'—'That's a point maturely

To be considered, ma'am ; and on your knees.

Just think of all the pomps and vanities,

And sinful lusts.   You know how Mary stands

At present—Could she be in better hands ?

A state's a state, regard it as you will—

Disturb that state, and who's responsible ? '

" ' Ah but,' she said, ' if Mr. Dynely come,

And want to marry her ? '   He looks as glum

As thunder—'When did Mr. Dynely say

He'd marry her at all ? ' and—'Let us pray ! '

He says, and knelt.   But those were words to pierce

The woman to the heart.   She stood up fierce
And stiff—she would not kneel: I got beside her,
And held her hand in mine.   The old man eyed her
With sad and wondering look.   The preacher frowned,
But prayed—when . . . suddenly . . . we heard a sound,
A sweet low tune—— 'twas in the room above—
O sir, my heart filled over—Love ! love ! love !
O love ! O death ! . . .

                But, sir, the preacher stayed,
He rose ; he listened 'Yes, it's sweet,' he said ;
' It's sweet ; she often sings like that, poor thing '
And hardly knows——' I felt the mother spring,
Although she didn't move--'Oh, is she crying ?'
I said—'Oh, is she, Mrs. Quayle ? or dying ?
Oh, dying ! dying ! Mrs. Quayle !'—'She may be,'
The woman said ; ' *that's* singing to her baby,
At any rate,' she said.   You see, she knew
The sort of sound, as if a baby drew
The song and suck at once—Ah, trust a mother
To tell that tune of tunes !   There is no other
Like that, of all the tunes—'She hasn't nursed
Her baby for a week : we feared the worst,'
The mother said.   ' But now—oh why, oh why

Are you so cruel ?   Sir, she need not die ;

She need not, Mr. King ! '

  She stopped ; the song

Continued—All at once—' I think we're wrong,

The old man said ; 'this lies beyond our power,'

And all his face was like a lovely flower—

' We'll go and tell her.'   Then he rose, and went ;

And with him went his wife.   The preacher bent

His head, and muttered something—didn't speak ;

I saw the tears were rolling down his cheek.

We left together—' In your prayers to-night

Remember me,' he said ; 'good-night ! good-night ! '

They're hard on human nature, bound to be ;

But still they can't get over it, you see.

" I heard next morning, when I gave a call

Up-street, that Mary wasn't pleased at all

With what I'd done—it took her unawares—

If people just would mind their own affairs,

She said, *it would be better—mind their own ;*

She only wanted to be left alone !

She wanted nobody to come and see her—

It was as Death had whispered in her ear

And spat into her mouth, and sucked her breath—

There is a kind of drunkenness of death

She'd got; she'd bathed her feet in death so long

That it had lost the chill: and Death is strong,

But Hope is stronger—— bully Hope! heart's-ease!

Sweet Hope, young Hope, that climbs upon the knees

Of Death, and hangs upon his neck! and so

I knew that it would be with her.   No, no!

We're not so fond of Death.

                     That very day

She nursed and nursed the little one, that lay

Upon her breast, a helpless snuggling bit

Of innocence.   They said her face was lit

With pride, if any one could call it pride—

Poor thing! and when she laid it at her side,

And raised herself, she kissed the little foot,

And talked of flowers, and where they should be put

To make the room look nice; and kissed her mother.

"Next day was Friday; then she couldn't smother

Her longing any more; she couldn't rest

A minute with them; wanted to be drest;

Sang to the baby, danced it, held it off

At arm's-length from her, till she made it cough

And blink; and then she nursed it for a while;

And then she lay quite peaceful—such a smile,

The mother said, and such a lovely bloom,

To see her tidying about the room!

And she would have the window open—yes—

The window—begged her mother with a kiss

To have the window open, so that she

Might hear the tug of paddles out at sea.

" The steamer came—I waited till the last—

No Dynely—no! I made the painter fast,

And jumped aboard the boat : I went below,

To see if he was there—but—Dynely?—no !

He hadn't come. I went ashore again ;

I saw the brothers standing at the lane ;

And, when they saw me by myself, they turned,

And walked away, they did. My head, sir, burned

With misery—O God of Israel !

And then . . . and then . . . I had to go and tell.

I made it look as likely as I could ;

He hadn't come ; but then of course he would—

Next boat, no doubt. And so they thought it better

That Mary should be told—*No doubt, a letter*
Had come by post—they'd have it in the morning :
And so, without the smallest bit of warning,
They told her—'Shut the window *now*,' she said :
And then her mother wrapt her in the bed,
And felt her all a tremble.

                      Morning came—

No letter, but the paper, and a name
That made me start—' Births, Marriages,' you know,
' Deaths . . . Herbert Dynely, Dynely Hall '—just so—
And, in another place, ' Sad accident.'
It seems, soon after I had left, he went
Far up the river to a place where rocks
Run out, and make a gully : two big blocks
Lean from each side, as if inclined to meet,
One higher than the other—fifteen feet
Of slant apart.   The downward jump was hard,
The up was worse ; and yet the man who dared
The one must dare the other : from the ledge
On which he stood the cliff was like a hedge
Behind him, six good fathoms, smooth as glass :
Below him, from the throttle of the pass,
Half choked with churning stones, the water slid

Into a deep black pool. The jump was called the
Strid.

"They found him in the pool, and people thought
He must have had a salmon on, and brought
His fish into the narrows. Then, you see,
He couldn't play him there; so jumps to free
His running tackle; doesn't do to jerk him—
Jump back again's the only way to work him—
Jumps, misses, strikes the crags, back, front, good God!
Stunned, bleeding, helpless, still he holds the rod,
And held it when they found him—dead enough—
Just where the water shoaled : the gear was tough ;
The salmon was below him, fast as glue—
The rascal—sulking, wondering what to do.

"So that's how Dynely died. This news was broke
To Mary very gently. No one spoke
But what they had to speak, and all combined
To be as helpful, and as good and kind
As ever they could be. But that strong love
Of Death came back upon her now, and strove
Against our kindness. Most of us, indeed,

Knew what must be the end : such strains exceed
The strength of human hearts.   Before she died,
She sent for me.   I stood at her bedside . . .
Bedside . . . bedside . . . O sir, the other hopes !
The other thoughts ! . . . O sir, man only gropes,
At best, through darkness : here, at last, was light—
But not of this world.

     'Twas a lovely sight,
But terrible . . . poor darling little bed—
Poor lamb ! poor dear !   But how I stooped my head
Against her lips to hear her whispering,
And what she said, that was not anything
But sweet low sighs—and what I could not say,
No matter how I tried, and came away,
And left her, when they told me. . . . Wait a bit . . .
That is . . . that must be. . . . O sir, *this* is it . . .
Young Dynely lies in Dynely church ; and she
Lies *there !* "

    He pointed where above the sea
Saint Maughold's Church lay girt with cross and rune
And grave. . . . Just then forth sailed the stately moon
Full orbed ; and, from a vista of retreat
Cloud caverned, lo ! a face divinely sweet

Looked forth, and, every fold distinct with light,

Soft garments floated on the field of night.

"Behold!" I cried, "O Richard mine, behold

The robe of silver, and the crown of gold!

See, see! she smiles!" Straightway the vision passed:

But Richard spoke not, only held me fast

By hand and arm—We rose, and down the slope

Walked silently—— O Love! O Death! O Hope!

BELLA GORRY

By the Pazon

Westward to Jurby, eastward if you look,
The coast runs level to the Point of Ayre,
A waste of sand, sea-holly, and wild thyme—
Wild thyme and bent.   The Mull of Galloway
Is opposite.   Adown the farthest west,
Not visible now, lie stretched the hills of Morne.

A cottage, did you say?   Yes, once it was;
A ruin now   the naked gables stand
Roofless—the walls are clay, save where round stones,
Picked from the beach, supply the mason's art
With base Cyclopean.   See the narrow hole
That served for window ! see the poor dead hearth.
This was the home of one whom, for the wealth

And strength of her great love, I call not poor—
Else, poor indeed.   The story of her life
You'd like to know ?   So far as known to me,
You shall—a simple story 'tis in sooth,
And somewhat sad.   Yet in the simple fact
God often speaks : and, as for sadness, sir,
I think such sadness is a thing most sweet.

The marriage tie, the household ordinance,
The regulated decencies, the home,
Are God's appointment—so to train a race
Healthy and strong ; yet can He nurture strength
And beauty in mere wildings—grace and joy,
Nay, goodness, and the firmest bond of love—
Firmer, it may be, for the sense in both
Of helplessness, of grave neglect, and scorn—
Firmer, as fastened in the absolute root
Of sheer maternity, where fatherhood
Is but the remnant of a weary dream.
So, while our gardens bloom, a humble flower,
Flung o'er the wall, may take the dews of God,
And breathe His air, and, in the wilderness,
Unfold the lovely splendour of a rose.

When Bella Gorry came to dwell amongst us,
She was not young.   Full thirty years, at least,
She'd seen : she was a stranger to us here,
A south-side woman.   We were harvesting
When first she came, and joined the shearers : none
Knew where she lived, or how; until, one night,
Passing among the bents, I heard a cry
As of a child, and heard the murmured song
Wherewith the mother sought to quiet it—
And this was Bella Gorry.   Round her rose
The swelling sand-heaps : it was in September,
A starlit night.   A fence of sods uptorn
Encompassed her ; and she had hollowed out
The sand, and made such shelter as she could.
But it was cold, and she had bowed her head
Over her babe, herself to sleep inclined—
And still the cry, and still the drowsy croon.

I stood amazed ; for in the Isle of Man
Our poor are not neglected.   You indeed
Must know such sights familiar : in the streets
And purlieus of great towns, the homeless wretch
Is never wanting, nor the country-side

Lacks its appropriate vagabond—the *tramp*,

Is't not? you call him—who in hedge or ditch

Lies hungry, gazing upward to the stars.

To him the state assigns a scanty dole,

Which he rejects. Not so with us—our poor

We deem God's charge, an individual care

To every Christian man, which whoso slights

God's ordinance slights—

        Therefore I stood amazed ;

And asked her who she was, and where her home.

She did not stir, but answered moodily—

"My name is Bella Gorry ; and I have

No home but this."—"Then come with me," I said ;

"The little one is cold : it is not fit

That you should lodge like this." But she no word

Replied ; only she tightened that close grasp

Wherewith she held the child ; and I could hear

Deep breathings of her breast, that seemed like sighs—

So that I knelt, and prayed. Then to my prayer

I knew that she attended. Nay, I prayed

In all humility : for now I felt

I was confronted with the deepest wrong

That man can do to woman, cause for shame

To me and all men.   So I prayed that God
Would pity us, and, in His wisdom, make
This wrong thing right ; give comfort to this heart
Nigh broken, and dispose her to remit
Her grief to Him, and to regard in me
His minister for such relief designed.

But vain my prayer, or seeming vain, for she
All proffered aid refused, and lifted up
At last her head, and, with unloving words,
Bade me be gone.   I went, but firm resolved
What I should do.   The earliest light of morn
Found me upon the field, where, one by one,
The shearers entered, till the field was full.
And Bella sheared—but she had left her babe
In that dry hollow far among the bents,
And ranged her with the shearers.   Then I spoke
To some I knew most apt, but chief to him,
The master of the farm, a soul full fraught
With love and active goodness.   He for me
A willing band detached.   I led them where
The child lay sleeping   in its little hands
Blue-bells fast clasped, and 'neath its head soft moss,

Plucked from the mooragh.   Then a little girl,

The farmer's daughter, took the child, and fed it

With milk, and nursed and danced it till it crowed.

But we with spade and pick unceasing worked

Till we had reared the framework of this cot

You see.   Nor did the mother know, before

Noon glowed, and, stealing from the harvest field,

She sought her child : and she was well content.

And when, or e'er the week was out, the roof

Stood thatched and necessary furniture

Of bed and board, by kindly hands supplied,

Was stored within, she saw, and the dull cloud

Broke ; and her soul was lightened, and she came

To me, and, with the rush of many tears,

Yet guarded by a fence of dignity,

How found I know not, she poured forth her thanks

And blessings.   So it was that Bella came

To dwell within my parish, and to be

My friend most loved, and worthy of my love.

This was her home ; for many quiet years

She lived within these walls, and had such peace

As theirs may be, whose purpose is to guard

One precious treasure, being all that's left.

It was a little girl that made her glad—

For she could yet be glad—a very star

To light her life : and well she tended it,

And saw it grow in beauty and in strength ;

And took it with her to the harvest field,

Or other work, as needs she must, who lived

A lonely woman.   I have seen the babe

Against a stook soft propped of drooping sheaves

Asleep, or, wakeful, gazing on the clouds ;

And I have noted how the field was hushed

In silence.   Only, ever and anon,

Some woman's heart would yearn for very love,

And make her quit her shearing rank a space,

To kiss this flower that smiled amid the corn.

Then would some strong man say—" Let me kiss too "—

But others said that it was naught, and murmured

Of *evil ways*, and *lightness not rebuked*,

And *sin encouraged*.   Still the baby smiled ;

And Bella reaped, and answered not a word.

So 'twas one day I came into the field
Where she was reaping, and I heard the voice
Of strong contention—it was Henry Tear,
My tenant—but you do not know the man—
He rents the glebe—a worthy soul enough,
And not ill-natured. What had angered him
They did not tell me; possibly some slackness
About the work, and how the women lost
Their time. He did not see me: hot and fierce,
I heard his last words only. Bella stood
Before him, pale and trembling—"Take the child
Away!" he said, "and bring it not again!
I will not have this bastard in my field."
And no one spoke.

          Then from behind the stook
I stepped, and took the little one, embraced,
As in the church I hold them at the font,
So by the altar of the golden sheaves
I held the child, and signed her with the cross,
And said Christ's words—ah, blessed, blessed words!
How we *should suffer them to come to Him,*
And not forbid them, for of such God makes
His kingdom. And I turned to Tear, and said—

" You must become even as this little child,

If you would enter heaven at the last.

Then let it lie, a little piece of heaven

Upon your field."

           But he was much rebuked,

And leaned his arms upon the hedge, and leaned

His face upon his arms, and strove to hide

His shame—and I remember it so well—

That is the field, high up upon the brow,

Near the cliff's edge—it was a lovely day,

But hot with hum of bees, and glare of sand,

And thunder, and the trouble of the shearing,

And Tear was angry; but I conquered him.

You smile—ah well—you are quite right—I'm not

A man to conquer—— anything, perhaps—

Nay, sir, the thing is so—and yet we have

Our little triumphs—little vanities,

No doubt, were better said; but God knows all—

Knows all—knows all - knows all. But think not,

     sir,

The little one was not baptized before,

And dedicate to God with holy rite.

'Twas but my parable, a way to reach

The good man's heart, for he was really good,
And felt it. So our little Sarah grew.

Now, as she grew, she lacked not, as beseemed
Her age, for sweet, or toy, or cap, or frock,
Gay ribbon, cloak as gay. Good Bella's store
Sufficed for all; nor would she have her child
Stinted of ought. It seemed as if, beside
Her love, she had a need of some delight
In form and colour, some embodiment
Of dreams, ideals, nurtured in the waste
Of hope forlorn, and purpose unfulfilled—
Imperfect turned to perfect, dark to dawn—
God's magic for great sorrows.
                                        So she wrought,
Instinctive artist, coveting the grace
Of utmost finish for the one pure gem
Saved from her life-wreck : so it seemed to me,
Much pondering how the sweet fantastic joy
Expanded to an outlet of constraint—
Uncertain—certain, simple recompense
Ordained of God for women who have loved
And lost, yet cherish beauty, knowing it

A good, although it has not been to them
A good.   To them a little child becomes
The glory of the prime, the incarnation
Of that which should have been, nay was, and is
For ever glowing in the secret depths
That feed the springs of action—from what type
Of mean inadequate idol caught, what hero
Proved unheroic, matters not, it seems,
Since love transfigures baseness.

                        You have seen them
Doubtless, these mothers—and you have observed
How fierce they often are, what stern regard,
What fire ascetic, jealous, watchful, burns
In her poor eyes, *who holds her babe a trophy*
Snatched fearful from the vanquished field of love,
And, as a trophy, decked.   No words of mine,
Dear sir, I beg to say—I mean, that flight
About the *trophy.*   'Twas Professor Jones
Of Oxford, reinforcing my poor speech
One day—Professor Jones - Professor Jones—
A very clever man.   But I rebuked him,
For, though we pity, we should not encourage,
Nor clothe with specious names what God has cursed.

Professor Jones was here?   Oh yes—you know him?
You are from Oxford? really! ah then
You'll understand how the Professor smiled
His weary Oxford smile, and said no more.

But I apologise.   I loved the child.
I loved her very much.   And I have gone
And watched the mother playing with her child,
Myself unseen, and marked the greediness
Of her great love ; until, one Saturday,
My sermon finished, ere the sun had set,
I went to Bella's cottage.   She had washed
The little one, and laid it like a pearl
Upon her breast.   Then I entranced beheld
The glory and the splendour of the babe,
And Bella lifted her upon the bed,
And asked that I would pray.   Then side by side
We knelt and prayed : and, as I prayed, I saw
The crimson flush that entered at the door
Pass straight between us to the sleeping child,
As it had been its angel.   When I rose,
Bella remained upon her knees, her face
Deep hidden in the coverlet, nor moved

Before I left.   O sir, what strange sweet throb
Surprised my heart!——— but these are difficult things.

So little Sarah grew, till she could run
Upon the shore, and gambol at my side.
And often, when her mother was a-field,
I'd find her all alone, but well content,
As trusted now to "keep the house," yet free,
At my proposal, to relax her care,
And scurry on the sand, and see my dog
Rush open-mouthed upon the waves, and bark,
And bark again—she loved to hear him bark.

And Sarah grew, and was no more a babe,
But a great girl.   Then more conspicuous seemed
Poor Bella's taste fantastic— certainly,
Fantastic— that was it- a string of beads,
Wreathed cunningly, a bow, a belt, the hair—
The everything so different, and then
The subtler difference that lay behind.
And she wore shoes the daintiest that are made,
And stockings violet, or, haply, pink,

Or blue—whereas our children here go barefoot.

And this gave much offence : our farmers' wives

Were angry at these *capers*—that's their word—

These ways eccentric, alien, scandalous—

They said the child was like *a gipsy child;*

They said the child was like a *monkey perched*

Upon a barrel-organ in the street,

Or some wild changeling, *draggled through a fair*

To dance, and smirk, and shake the tambourine,

And grow to be a wanton—so they said.

But I, to whom the unfamiliar garb

Seemed not excessive, wedded, as it was,

To modesty, and scrupulous cleanliness—

I could not blame it ; nay, it had a charm

For me, a charm of novelty and grace—

The break of dull monotony ; as if

Some day among the gulls upon the beach

I should perceive a bird of paradise,

Or mark a fire-fly in the dusky bents.

Yet, when the little one was old enough

To come to school, and I had fixed the day,

And all was ready, I had many fears—

Indeed I all but asked to see her dressed
That morning, ere she left her mother's hand,
But did not venture : only, when she came,
I bade the mistress thoroughly examine
Each hem, and stitch, and gore, and plait, and seam,
And, if need be, abate, or modify.
Moreover I contrived to bring two friends,
Lady parishioners, mature in years,
Into the school that day : who, when they saw,
Approved, and were surprised : the child was dressed
Like other children, only wondrous neat—
Indeed, sir, I was thankful, recognising
The plastic spirit of my humble friend,
And how she caught the cue of circumstance.

So all was well, and Sarah grew apace,
And was an excellent scholar, apt and good.
And she had much of native dignity,
And calm control, well suited to abash
Our rougher lads : and, even before she left
The school, she looked so stately and so pure,
So sweetly tolerant, and yet so firm
Of principle, being resolute for good

Above all else, that evil things withdrew

From off her virgin path; and vulgar phrase,

And gesture loose, nor any wicked act,

Could e'er approach her—happy, happy such—

O sir, how happy! who, as in the sphere

Of their own crystal purity contained,

Are *naturally* safe, and, effortless,

Compel the baser elements—how few,

God knows. For is it not a weary strife

With most of us, our peace, if peace we have,

The fruit of mere exhaustion?—ah, God knows—

And God knows too—but 'tis a happier knowledge—

What preparation in the silent depths

Of these white, virginal souls is made, what conflict,

Perhaps, of other essences, to them

External, viewless powers, keeps beating back

The incursive ill, and still unbroken holds

That limited space wherein they walk secure—

So in the moving centre of a storm

There is a core of quiet, is there not?

In such a place as this, I need not say,

The children at our school cannot remain

Beyond the term prescribed by homely needs,

And exigence of labour.   Sarah stayed

Up to her sixteenth year, a privilege

Not many of our working class obtain,

For her by Bella eagerly desired,

And jealously protected—and the girl

Made rapid progress, justifying all.

And, when she left, her mother would not take her

To work upon the fields, as she herself

Was wont, but sought a place of service for her

In Ramsey, with a family genteel,

Yet staid, and sober, which from Liverpool

Had come to spend the summer : and with them,

When they returned to Liverpool, she went,

To be their servant in that awful place.

But, ere she went, we had our Confirmation ;

And Sarah came to be prepared by me :

And she impressed me much as one well girt

With Christian armour; and her frame of mind

Was excellent.   Her answers, whether spoken,

Or written, such as I myself indeed

Would not have been ashamed of ; and, in truth,

Her hand was always wonderfully clear.

So I was pleased : but Bella troubled me.

    Her tendency to gauds broke out afresh

On this occasion, seeming to have died

As she grew old ; or, possibly, her daughter

Had mitigated it, with exquisite tact,

Suggesting compromise, and ever holding

A mean, that had a pathos of its own,

So happily did she propitiate

Her mother's foible, subtly indistinct

In her distinction—as she managed it.

But now dear Bella hankered for a cap,

So frizzed, beribboned, done about with lace

And gauze, wherewith her daughter should appear

Before the Bishop, that I knew his lordship

Would be quite scandalised.   Debate ran high

For quite a week between herself and me :

And I was vexed.   But Sarah made it right—

Yet not without some risk of public blame—

She wore no cap at all ; and never, sir,

Was Bishop's hand laid on a lovelier head.

So Sarah was confirmed, and went to England ;
And Bella had no doubts ; she knew her child.
Nor is there any tragedy behind
My simple story—ruin, sir, and death—
Thank God ! it was not thus, and could not be—
I say, *thank God !* for I have known of many
Caught in the snares of your great Liverpool,
Burned in the fire of your great Liverpool,
Cast forth like ashes on the unhallowed streets
Of your great Liverpool.　An awful place
I said it was ; and so it is to us,
To us, sir, anxious for our children's good,
Our children's life.　Oh yes ! I know there are
Good men in Liverpool, else Sodom's doom
Had fallen upon her long ago, who asks
The annual tribute of our shame—pollutes,
Devours—O God ! to think of it is death !

Good men in Liverpool—yes, sir, oh yes -
Undoubtedly—I know some clergymen
In Liverpool, who are most excellent,
Most admirable men in every way—
There's Mr.　　I forget his name　　his church

Is somewhere—— really I can't remember—
You see, your Liverpool is such a place,
Enormous, is it not? and most confusing.
You think I'm prejudiced—perhaps I am—
But you'll allow it is confusing, sir,
Confusing to a stay-at-home like me—
Well, well—I do not like your Liverpool.

But Sarah was not easily confused:
She could walk steadily where others swerve
And stagger from the track.   Her feet were firm
And supple with the elasticity
Of innocence and maidenly resolve—
God giving her strength, God answering our prayers,
Refreshing her according to her need,
Nay, filling her with light; so that each year,
When she came back to see us, she was good,
And absolutely incorrupt as ever—
Unchanged indeed, save only that sweet change
Which comes of larger life, more copious flow
Of impulse ever chastened, broader space
Of soul, reflecting more variety
Of forms—as when a little mountain stream

Swims out into the figure of a lake,

And mirrors all the sky, and all the clouds.

Such change was added beauty, perfect joy,

And balance of a heart that knew no fear—

Sarah was fearless; that you saw at once—

Yet so affectionate, and simply kind.

It was a real little festival

When she came home to see us: every face

Was brighter for her look, such interest,

And such excitement, in the parish here!

For half a mile upon the Ramsey road

The people from the cottages came out,

And waited for the cart, the Parson's cart,

Which always brought her from the boat.   Indeed

The first time that she came I did not care

To be among them: but the second time

I lingered at the corner of the lane;

And when they saw me, all, with one consent,

But tacitly, held back, as though they thought

It was for me to welcome her.   And so

It came to be a custom of the place;

And I was always there, and nothing loth

Such little things make up our round of life,
And are the landmarks of its quiet course ;
And are not very little, after all,
For those who value simple loyalty,
And have respect for unpretending worth.

It was a pleasant and a happy scene :
But most 'twas happy, most 'twas pleasant, sir—
To me at least 'twas most—to see how Bella,
From mid-day till the twilight brought her hope,
Upon a sandhill, which advanced to meet
The road, sat spotless in the mere perfection
Of cap and kerchief, conscious of her hearth
Clean swept, and all the cottage bright as glass.
And so for hours she sat, most patiently
Knitting : and, now and then, some one would come—
Most frequently myself—and change a word
Of cheer, and in the very quiet of her tone
Divine the gathered loneliness, that now
Expected recompense, as justly due
To all those wintry longings in the night.
But when the sunset came, and that great joy
Was imminent, then Bella's needles clicked

Irregular, and from her trembling hands
Slipped devious, and her face was fixed upon
The long white road, and from her eyes dropped tears.
Then came the cart; and on my aiding hand
Sarah leaped light, but Bella waited still:
And we went up to her.   So, every year,
It grew to be a custom, as I said,
A ritual of observance most exact,
Which changed, the people would have been amazed.

A Sabbath time for Bella, be assured—
A blessed, blessed time! and Sarah brought
Such presents for the children all about
That everywhere the little ones rejoiced,
And followed her.   But chiefest bliss to me
Was in the evening, when the day was fine,
That sacred week, for well it might be called so,
While Sarah stayed with us, to see them walk,
The mother and her child, upon the shore,
At distance I, yet near enough to note
The close embrace of interwoven arms,
Slow step harmonious, stately forms erect,
Yet flowing in accordant tenderness—

Tall women both, yet Bella was less tall
Than Sarah, grown to perfect womanhood.

Nine years had passed, and still our Sarah served
In the same house.   But, when the tenth year came,
Came news that Sarah was to be a wife
Before she saw us next—a man well off,
Intelligent, respectable, who loved her,
And whom she loved—you know the sort of man—
Connected with some—oh, a worthy man—
Should be her husband; and from marriage bells
Forthwith they twain would cross the sea, and make
Some stay with us—so Sarah's letter said.
But Bella, whatsoe'er she felt, was silent:
Only I thought I saw a heavy look—
And yet perhaps I did her wrong; for how
Could prospect of so great a change not throw
A shadow on her life? which having passed,
Bright sunshine would succeed.   A mother's heart—
'Tis a great mystery, sir, a mother's heart.

And now the day approached that they should come;
And Bella seemed as if an inward strife

S

Had ended, and her soul was left in peace:
And she addressed her to the patent needs
Of service, and all hospitable cares.
And, when they came, I could not but rejoice
To mark how radiant Sarah looked, to see
Her husband too, a handsome man, well-grown,
Well-set; kind, honest face, and honest speech,
Where haply failed an aitch, as reason would,
But nothing failed of modesty and truth:
Content, I grasped his hand.

                    Then Bella asked
If, that one night, in her old cottage home,
She might have Sarah to herself   "You were
My architect," she said to me, "you know
How far accommodation serves."   Whereat
Her husband not surprised, we speedily
Arranged that he should at the Vicarage
Be entertained, my guest.   We supped with her,
Then left them.   'Twas a pleasant night of stars,
And murmuring ripples, and sweet drowsy winds,
That scarcely stirred a leaf.   And I was glad
To make the acquaintance of our Sarah's husband.
And as we walked and walked: and I could see

That he was *most* intelligent,—acquainted
With much that lay beyond my beat—the arts
Of busy life, and ways of toiling men,
And springs of wealth and industry—

       We walked,
And still the light was in the window, still
They did not sleep, and it was getting late.
Then he to me—" I will draw near, and know
What holds them watching : " to the window stept,
And looked a while, then beckoned me approach,
But silently ; and I approached. Then he—
" Dear sir, you are a clergyman. In God's name
I bid you see the sight that I have seen."

 Then through the opening of the narrow pane
I gazed, and saw how Bella had undressed
Her child, as long ago, when she and I
Had prayed beside the little one. But now
It was the absolute omnipotence
Of woman's beauty given to my view,
As in some wondrous dream : for Bella knelt,
And clasped the marble of her daughter's knees,
And kissed the softness of her daughter's breast,

And drank the music of her daughter's voice,
And seemed to take assurance of each sense
That this dear child, thus come to full estate
Of bodily form, was her own little one,
Flesh of her flesh, the same that she had born
And nursed in sorrow, now complete in joy.

Oh *physically*, sir, it was supreme—
This Sibyl clinging to this Venus.   Nay,
You'll pardon my poor fancy—classical,
Perhaps—but that is not the point—those faces,
Those faces, sir—that worship, and that smile—
Love! if this was not love, then where is love?
The love, the smile, the face, sir—either face—
Both faces in an ecstasy of love.
" Nursing the baby "—so I said to him,
Who yet again would look, and look again:
But came with me at last; and, reft of speech,
And in our hearts the murmuring of deep awe,
We sought the Vicarage; and, ere we slept,
I prayed for all.

                    Next morning, when I rose,
I found him up, and ready to descend

To Bella's cottage.   At the opened door
Stood Sarah, very quiet.   In her eyes
Methought I saw a trouble; but she spoke
Her greeting with a voice that seemed unmoved :
Then bade us enter.   Which when we had done,
She gently turned the coverlet; and there
Lay Bella, with a sunbeam on her brow,
A bright young sunbeam—Bella, sir, was dead.

Of course, the doctors called it heart-disease—
But who can tell?   God took her to Himself;
He knows the time——   But I neglect my function—
Westward to Jurby, eastward, as I said,
The coast runs level to the Point of Ayre.

THE END

Printed by R. & R. CLARK, *Edinburgh.*

www.ingramcontent.com/pod-product-compliance
Lightning Source LLC
Chambersburg PA
CBHW020347030726
47496CB00007B/2037